The Electric Minute

The Electric Minute

Farley L. Dunn

Volume I

THREE SKILLET

THE ELECTRIC MINUTE, Dunn, Farley L.
1st ed.

Vol. 1

 THREE SKILLET

www.ThreeSkilletPublishing.com

ISBN: 978-1-943189-50-2

What happened to the FLASH in everyday FICTION?

_____

30 brain-busting reads in three minutes or less to

jumpstart your imagination.

Table of Contents

The Newly Undead

I DIDN'T MEAN to kill her.

Then, all things considered, I guess you need to see that night my way. Things hadn't gone well. Ha! You can say that again. I'd lost nearly thirty grand in a poker game, and my pockets were coming up dust. I had my silver monogrammed letter opener that I always carried, and it was getting pretty lonely in my jacket pocket.

Then she came on to me like a fly to honey, sitting in my lap like a hired party girl at a randy stag party. I'd seen her at the bar, earlier, name of Selina. She'd caught my eye, and I'd bought her a drink.

I liked her, too.

Except for the money thing, it would have turned out to be a good night. A very good night. We'd have gone back to my hotel suite—one at the top of the tower, the kind where the really ritzy gamblers have all their dreams come true—and I would have worried about the hotel bill I could no longer cover come sunrise.

We didn't make it that far.

Not even close.

It was Jack the Crack that tried to put the cinch on my plans. Well, on our plans, because by that time, she had her hand inside my shirt, working its way to places you don't need to know. She was licking my ear, and I was bleary-eyed with her presence. I was in the middle of my final hand, ready to give up for the night, when the Crack laid out his cards, grinned at me, and his gold tooth caught the light.

"Your girl, you willing to wager a night with her?"

His words were a bass guitar in apoplectic overload, just at the threshold of hearing, and I caught the insinuations. He'd thrown a knife-thrust of insults in that one sentence, and my mind went crazy with the need to protect Selina's reputation.

A woman I didn't even know.

I should have shrugged it off, thrown my cards onto the table, and walked away. That would have been the smart thing to do. Still, no one's ever accused me of being smart around women and made it stick. Besides, her hand was so deep into my shirt, I didn't know how she could reach so far.

I forgot my dusty pockets, and I fired back, with all the snarling arrogance I could manage, "Joker's wild."

The cards flashed in the dim light, and it seemed magic happened at that moment. With her as my stake, I pulled aces in every hand, dealt one after another. She cheered by clapping her hands, and more than once, she kissed me on the cheek. I couldn't lose. The Crack was furious, with his face growing redder with each hand he lost.

I just kept raking the chips my way and setting them aside. I was going to be a rich man after tonight.

"Let's go."

She whispered the words in my ear, and

I looked up from my royal flush to catch a glimmer in her eyes that said she had plans that wouldn't wait. Desire swept through me, and I didn't care about the money anymore. I glanced at the Crack and flipped the cards his direction.

"This hand's yours. You've lost enough." I stood, and she wrapped herself around me like I was a pole and she was a dancer, and she was about to give the performance of her life.

"You don't want to leave with Selina." The Crack spat the words, pushing my cards away. His eyes were coals as he taunted me. "You play well. Let me save your life tonight."

"Fool. You've given me my life tonight. I intend to live it up on your cash." Selina's hand was toying with my waistband, and I wanted to get her alone and to myself as fast as I could.

"Ache, your life! Waste it if you want. Come play again after the woman sucks you dry."

Everyone at the table went silent at his words, but I didn't pay attention. She was licking my neck, and I had my arm around her waist. She felt good, too, like a piece of candy that I wanted to consume until it was all gone.

We made it as far as the elevator. Once inside, she ripped my shirt wide, tearing the buttons off on the way down, like a hungry beast. It was half a grand, but what was money? I figured I'd won two million from Jack. What was $500 against that?

I hardly felt the prick of her teeth. They say the bite of a bat doesn't hurt because it emits an analgesic that erases the pain. I think love does the same. All I knew was my knees went weak, and I sank to the floor of the elevator as she held me in her arms.

I was so far gone that I didn't hear the ding of the door as it opened to let her out.

When I awoke, I knew what she'd done. I was hungry, so hungry, and every warm neck drew me like a fly to honey. I wanted a taste of every man, woman, and child so badly I could barely make my way to my room.

That's why I killed her. I found my silver letter opener in my pocket, and I knew what I had to do. I discovered her back at Jack's table, her hand inside another man's shirt. Silver kills as well as wood, when it's driven into the heart.

Now, I'm the one undead, and Jack's looking my direction. I've got a mark to play, and then I get to feed.

Second Chances

THE AIR TURNED black all around me.

It wasn't like it was nighttime or anything. That would have made sense.

I glanced in my rearview mirror to make sure no one was barreling up on me and flipped my blinker to pull to the side of the road. Heck, how would I know if they were there? There'd been no warning—like they couldn't predict the sun was going out—and I sure hadn't had time to turn my lights on. What made me think anyone else would be quicker to the draw than me?

I did find the switch as my tires dropped

off the pavement and onto the dirt. Even with the burst of light, I could tell by the feel of the car, that slight shifting from asphalt to sand that comes with pulling off the road. Almost slippery, if sand and grass can be said to possess those qualities.

I got out and looked around. The car was running, loud in the moment, and I reached inside and killed it. When I stood back up, I noticed the silence. Nothing. I was only three blocks from the shore, and the sea should be pounding the coastline, whether it was night or day.

Especially since it was still mid-afternoon, if I measured the time by the clock.

I listened for seagulls to no avail. The channel buoys were silent, too, but then, they would be, if there weren't any waves. I bet I wouldn't hear the bleat of the ferry, either. Ever. Not unless the light came back.

If it ever did.

I don't know why I thought that. It just seemed logical that the world had changed in a way that was life-altering, and my existence wasn't returning to what it used to be.

Not that it was something I minded. Not with the collapse of the company, and Mindy walking out on me. Heck, even my car was about to be repossessed. I hadn't made a payment on it in three months, and the repo company had been hovering at the end of my block like a vulture in line for a good meal. Only the property's electric gates had kept them at bay this long.

I felt something brush my face, and a shiver ran down my spine. Words . . . a whisper in the wind. Except there was no wind.

I shivered, this time with my whole body.

I pulled my key from the dash and slammed the door. I felt for the road and began to walk toward the ferry landing. Maybe I'd be lucky and catch a ride. They'd have lights, and they ran the channel, rain or shine, night or day. No simple blackout would stop the ferry from making its scheduled run.

I'd gone about five steps and was still in range of the car's lights when I stopped. The car door. I'd slammed it, and it hadn't made a sound.

Weird wasn't the word for what this

was.

I called out, "Hey!" I smiled. My voice worked. I was just preoccupied, I guessed, and hadn't paid attention.

The wind whispered to me again, and I grew cold. It had been hot before, a good day to come to the island and wind up a life that had become riddled with disasters so big there was no use in trying to patch it back together. That was my intent. Take a last day on the beach, try to remember when life had been good, and then let it all go.

No one would find me there, as this was the end of summer, and the beach house was already locked up for the season. By spring, there'd be nothing left to find, except the remains of what I'd once been.

Then, with Mindy gone, who'd come to look? The Trust would pay the upkeep for another year, the end of the season would come again, and there I'd be, vanished, with no one to care.

I brushed a tear back, and I realized I couldn't see the car's headlights any longer. I was walking by memory, a route I'd traveled since I was a boy. I remembered a girl I'd summered with on the island, Veronica. I'd fallen in love with her at thirteen and promised to marry her when we were grown.

Mindy had gotten in the way, and I'd lost track of my first love. It was the beginning of the disasters that had tried to gobble up my life, and they'd well-nigh succeeded. Look at me, on a dark road in the middle of the day, walking to a ferry I couldn't see, so that I could end my life in the comfort of dead and exhausted memories with no one else around me.

The touch on my face came again, but this time it was more. I felt my gut twist inside, and pain shot through my knees. I crumpled, writhing in agony. Somehow, as I cried out, I wondered why I'd walked. I had the keys in my pocket. I could have driven to the ferry.

Maybe stupid was why my life was falling apart.

Then a high-pitched whine filled the air, and a bright light surrounded me.

"Defibrillator charging . . . shocking patient now!"

The air went black again, and silence engulfed everything. After what seemed forever, I felt something brush my face, and a voice whispered to me.

"Jerry, can you hear me? Open your eyes, if you can. You were in a car wreck. We thought . . . we thought we'd lost you."

"Mindy?" I struggled to open my eyes.

"No, silly. It's Veronica, your wife. The kids are outside, and they want to see you. I'm so glad you're safe. We couldn't bear to lose such a wonderful man."

My vision cleared as my children tumbled into the room, with beautiful Veronica corralling them so they didn't overwhelm me. Sun streamed through a window. I smiled as tears ran down my face. I planned to live in the sunshine from now until the day I died.

And that was going to be a very long way away.

The Witching Hour

ICY FINGERS GRIPPED my arm in the darkness.

The cheers of the crowd filled the air around us, and we stood as the victorious team running across the artificial turf far below erupted into a mob, congratulating each other on a game well done. The field became a tumult of undulating bodies, as the back-slapping and hooting turned into the sound of the moment.

"You called it again."

I turned at the words, looking into my wife's face, and found a puckish grin smirking at me.

"You thought I wouldn't?" I returned

her tease as I adjusted my collar higher. The wind had picked up, and it was cold in the late evening. The game had started at eight, and it was now past eleven. We had less than an hour left. Soon we would be forced to head home, and all this would become a distant memory.

Distant memory. I smiled at that, and Darci smiled back, as she slipped on her gloves.

"It's a special treat, being here tonight. I want to congratulate you on winning the contest and earning this vacation."

"I couldn't have done it without you." I wrapped my arms around her in an old-fashioned hug, wondering if it would be caught on the large screens that displayed ebullient fans still in a celebratory mode. It was something we'd looked forward to, perhaps seeing ourselves in the history books of the era. *Couple Celebrates Team Victory with a Kiss!* Yeah, something like that. Wouldn't that be the best end to a wonderful day?

Then the fireworks began, flinging brilliant, eye-watering streams of color into the air behind the tiers of seats, and erupting into colorful flowers, spreading their petals into the moonless sky.

"This is what I came for." My wife's eyes glowed, and I could see the colored lights reflected in the moisture filling her eyes. "I've never seen fireworks. Not really."

In between clips of the pinwheeling explosives on the giant screens, couples appeared, waving at the cameras when they saw their images. Just down from us, a redhead with flowing locks over a team jacket began to wave at nothing, and when we looked, yes, there she was on the display, holding up her hands, with one gloved and a team banner in the other.

"I remember her," I remarked, as I pulled Darci closer. Her hair smelled good, and I tried to draw it in. I didn't know hair could smell so exquisite, and I didn't want to forget this moment, none of it, not the sounds of the crowd, the smell of the burning sulfur from the fireworks—and the rotten egg stench that made it real—or the feel of Darci's pleasure as she soaked it in.

"Look, this is why we're here." Darci

motioned with her gloved hand to the far side of the stands. "It's about to happen."

I felt a shiver of fear. A thrill was more like it. Had we chosen the correct side of the facility? When the flames erupted, would we be caught up in them? Or would we arrive home safely, just another anniversary trip to a time and place we'd never been before?

Some people died on these trips, after all.

That's when I saw us, up on the screen. We looked perfectly normal, a happy couple out for the evening, taking in the game, and exultant in our team's win. I leaned in and gave Darci a kiss, all the while keeping an eye on the screen. It had to look perfect, just like the old video reels showed. We'd assured our sponsors no one would notice our presence. We'd be a fly on the wall of history, and nothing in the future would change.

Then the stands behind us erupted into chaos, as one of the giant shells, unexploded, landed three rows back. People began to scramble as they yelled warnings to their companions.

"No!" Darci jerked away, pulling free

of my grasp. "We got it wrong. We're on the wrong side of the stadium. Run, Dan!" As she turned, she caught her foot and stumbled, falling to her knees.

I knelt at her side and inspected her ankle. It was red, and it would soon blacken into a deep purple. I'd seen it before. I glanced back to the screen, and there we were, left for all the world to see by a distracted camera operator. Or maybe he'd seen the shell and hoped to catch the action, perhaps win an award for Best Catastrophe Caught on Camera. I tried to remember if there had been one of those after the accident, but it wasn't something I'd researched.

"Dan?" Darci's face was red, and she looked at me with desperate eyes. I glanced at my watch, an old-fashioned affectation, but appropriate for the era.

"Three minutes to twelve." I smiled. "Explosions happened on both sides of the stadium, and it took four minutes for this side to collapse in flames. Here, I'll keep you safe."

"You'd better. I have work in the morning, and I can't afford to be late. I still owe for my share of this trip. I didn't get to come for free."

"Don't worry." I glanced at my watch. A minute had passed. I indicated the screen, to see my hand motioning. It was funny, in a way. "We're about to transition. Don't move until we get home."

Then, on the screen, just behind us, the shell erupted into a furious ball of flame. I could be seen watching my wrist, and just as the timepiece clicked over to midnight, we disappeared from the monitor, as the flames rolled past where we had been.

Just like the history books showed.

Passing Time

IT FELT LIKE something was watching me.

I stepped around the first tombstone, bypassing it, and I peered through the gloom. The sun was shining brightly—elsewhere, just not here—and I still had on my shades. I reached to my face, brushed aside an invisible spider web, and slipped the glasses aside.

A movement to the side caught my attention, and I studied the dappled sunlight, more shade than sun. In the darkest areas, it was nearly night. A leaf, surely. It was fall, after all. The cooling weather always brought down the leaves.

I relaxed, certain it was nothing. Graveyards were my thing. I had paper and charcoal in my satchel for rubbings. I framed them and sold them in my shop, and occasionally my boyfriend used them to create tee shirt designs. Halloween. Parties. That sort of thing.

The second tombstone held as little interest for me as did the first. I'd seen it featured on a webpage for people like me. Grave surfers. Stone foodies. Followers of those who'd already checked out of life.

Besides, it told the tale of an old woman who'd lived a full life. She was probably tired when she went. How boring was that? I liked the ones who died in their twenties, or their teens, imagining them to be snatched in their prime. They were the jet-setters, the rule-breakers, the ones who had lived a full life, even if they died in their youth.

How does that old song go? Only the good die young. I hoped none of these had died young, even if they were seventeen, or nineteen, or twenty-four.

I was deep into the cemetery, under a moss-encrusted oak, when I found my first prize. Born in 1933 and left the earth in 1946. How sad, I thought, as I knelt in the roughly mown grass and flipped open my satchel. I traced the letters etched into the stone. My pulse quickened as I imagined how this life had gone. Born at the end of the Great Depression, just as the economic fortunes of the country were about to change, perhaps in a grand house that had fallen into ruin along with the family's finances, this boy? girl? going by the name of Temper Petrous had played along dusty corridors amid the tattered furniture of a luxurious life gone to seed.

Why did thirteen-year-olds die, I mused, as I placed the paper on the stone and lifted my charcoal in my hand. The sound of a bird filtered through the trees, and I found it on a low branch. A Yellow Warbler. I was surprised to see it so far north. I would have expected a Tennessee Warbler, or a Blue-Winged variety. Must have been last week's storm that carried it out of its range.

No matter, the sound was pretty. It was probably what had spooked me earlier, the bird arriving, shifting branches and giving me the heebie-jeebies in the process. I shrugged and turned my attention back to the job at hand. I hoped to complete a dozen of these today. This place was a gold mine, so far off the beaten track that I was certain no one had dared venture past the first row of weathered stones. It was prime pickings for my shop, original designs that would sell like hotcakes to the right crowd.

Aligning the paper, I pressed the charcoal to the surface and swiped it sideways, letting the black pick up the varied texture of the stone. It made a pretty design, with the stone badly weathered into a rough semblance of the polished granite it had once been. My charcoal caught where the name dipped into the stone, and a black streak crawled across the paper.

Dang, I thought. At least I had plenty of paper to spare.

Still, I'd finish this one, and I'd know better how to improve the second version. I worked steadily but quickly to bring out the dates, wishing the stone carver had thought to tell whether the child was a boy or a girl. Temper. Who knew? It could be either one.

The second copy surprised me. Between the two rubbings, the texture seemed different.

Rougher. I thought of the warbler and looked for it. The branch it had been on was thicker than I remembered, heavier with leaves and nearly dragging the ground. Odd, I thought, but didn't think too much of it. I wasn't here for the trees, so they didn't count for much to me.

I finished that one and moved on, finding another gravestone to admire, this person only twenty when he passed on. *Beloved Athlete and Favorite Son.* How sweet. An outdoorsman, doing what he loved when he met his maker. That's what I wanted my tombstone to say, that I died doing what I loved. There couldn't be a better ending to a life well lived.

The deeper I got into the graveyard, the farther it seemed to extend. I looked back to the entrance, and I couldn't find it, anymore. The trees were taller, thicker than they'd seemed when I entered, but then, that was probably a trick of the light.

I noticed that the dates were more recent, so I must be in the newer section. Several headstones even had quirky death dates, ones that hadn't even happened. I rubbed one, just for laughs. Who inscribed a death on a tombstone when it hadn't occurred, yet?

The afternoon grew long, and I felt I hadn't eaten in a hundred years. Besides, I'd used up my last sheaf of paper, and my final charcoal was worn to a nub. I worked my way back to the entrance, only to find the gate rusted shut. I worked it free and stepped through.

I felt suddenly old. I slipped my satchel from my shoulder, to find the leather cracked and worn. It split, and my rubbings fluttered free, old, yellowed, and faded. The skin on my hands began to shrivel, and I could barely breathe, as I collapsed to the ground.

The Yellow Warbler I'd seen earlier—its distant descendant, I now realized—landed beside me and chirruped a funeral dirge as I crumbled into dust, leaving only weathered bones to mark that I'd been there at all.

Catching Her Eye

THE EYES IN the painting followed Eli.

Never mind they were just oil and pigment, something smeared across the canvas, an artist's rendition of an old soldier's sour expression that would forever haunt the mansion's dark walls.

He felt it every day on the way to breakfast, then back again. At lunch, they tracked his every move, and during the dinner hour, they judged his attire as appropriate or not, even if he wore the same thing every day.

He tried watching them from time to time, staring at the oil-formed orbs, but was frustrated at every turn. When he glared at the eyes, they looked away, as if daring him to accuse them of a misdeed most profound.

Now he hunched his shoulders and turned his head, refusing to look. It wasn't fair in his own home, but what choice did he have?

None, none at all.

Then Sally came to visit.

She was a happy presence in the formal parlors. Her smile brightened everything, and she wore laughter in her eyes. She was a friend of a friend, a sister, really, to someone, from what he heard, and he made excuses for her to return. It was the third party of the summer before he realized he was falling in love.

Eli hoped Sally was, too.

There were moments in the garden when she stopped to talk to him. Intimately, too, touching his arm and whispering to him how much she appreciated her invitation. Once, at a formal lunch, she sat across from him at the table, and her foot bumped his under the flowing cloth. She seemed puzzled at first, then caught his eye and gave an embarrassed laugh. She flushed a light rose just at her collar, and he didn't see that it could have been an accident.

Her attention made him want her more.

One Thursday Eli invited Sally for afternoon tea. He made sure no other invitations were out in the village, that the church calendar was clear, the ladies' auxiliary wasn't having a meeting, and there were no shops running specials that must be attended. He was clear she was under no compunction to attend, but her presence would be welcome, and it would help fill his empty day.

It was the first time he noticed her attention on the painting. She strolled by and seemed to smile at the scowling soldier's face, and she gave a little laugh, as if a moment of secret understanding had passed between them. Then she looked away, offered her arm, and they continued into the solarium for light cakes and an hour of pleasant conversation.

Eli forgot the incident, as when she slipped on her gloves afterward, she asked if she could return. His next party? he inquired with a smile.

Tea, tomorrow, Sally returned.

And so they did, letting it become a

daily habit. Her presence filled him with such warmth that he felt no concern when she made a point to visit the solitary soldier for a few moments each time she passed him by. Eli no longer felt the eyes following him as he made his way to breakfast, lunch, or dinner, and he knew why.

It was love.

That special attraction had entered the walls of his home, that emotional bond that draws people together, and all else is eclipsed from their souls. With the joy he now felt, he dismissed all the years of dread passing the painting as no more than an affectation on his part. Eyes following him? Bah! How foolish he'd been. It was loneliness that had haunted him, not dabs of pigment and a painter's brush strokes.

He felt emboldened one afternoon, and over decorative sandwiches, during a lull in the conversation, he remarked on the painting, noting that she seemed to find it fascinating. He laughed, telling her that at one time, he had felt that the eyes followed him.

Her reply surprised him. *You, too?*

Not anymore, Eli remarked and smiled,

although he didn't tell her why. The inquiry had been more a manner of connection, a point of conversation, something to let her know he was intimately aware of her moods and interests.

It was his way of saying he had fallen in love.

That night, preparing for the following evening's gala, Sally's words began to gnaw at him. *You, too?* What did she mean? It was just a painting. The eyes didn't *move*. They couldn't. Besides, he'd studied them closely numerous times, never once finding evidence to support the claim.

His feeling had been that, only, an emotional state of mind devastated by his desperate need for a companion in life and in love. His proof? He had found love, and the eyes no longer followed him.

He vowed to tell Sally of his desire for her the very next evening.

She arrived with a press of guests in the fading evening light, her bright laugh and her brilliant smile lighting the doorway. She paused for a very long time in front of the painting, with a look of longing in her eyes.

The gala continued around her.

As the evening wound down, Eli searched for her to tell her of his love, and she was nowhere to be found.

Eli finally located Sally the next morning.

The old soldier's eyes in the painting no longer followed Eli, even as he grew lonely and old. They were on the woman in the painting beside him, one with a very bright smile and eternal laughter in her eyes.

Birds of Pray

A SHRILL CRY echoed in the mist.

Off to the side, a stream tumbled down a rocky crevice, sending a spray of water droplets into the morning air.

It was early and cold, and Franklin slipped his hands into his pockets and wrapped them around the hand warmers he had broken open hours before. Warmth surged through his skin, and his shivering stopped. He would want his gloves on before they started up the mountain.

"Tchang, it seems we have company." Franklin watched the birds, eagles, he thought, although not Bald. No, not here in Patagonia. Their range didn't reach to the southern extremes of the Americas. It had to be another sort.

"Buzzard, sir." The aide, a guide native to the area, held a hand to his brow, shading, even though there was no sun.

"Come, Tchang. I may not know my birds, but I do know buzzards. That's no buzzard."

"My apologies. A buzzard-eagle, Black Chested, I believe. It's quite usual hereabouts." Tchang dropped his hand and turned away, already finished with the conversation. He had loaded Franklin's pack, and he was working on his own.

"Ah. So, I've learned something new. Carrion eaters, are they? Our Baldie is, from up north. They do like live food, though. I can't imagine what they would find up here. No life around that I've seen."

He was correct. They were above the tree line, and the landscape was rugged rock and occasional scree. They had crossed rotten patches of shale two days past, slowing them down. Today was their day to summit. Summer was almost gone, and the wind that was biting today would soon turn deadly, forcing everyone from the highest peaks.

"Sir?" Tchang touched Franklin on the elbow, his careful motion showing a certain amount of deference and respect. "Shall we?"

He had his pack on his back, and the smaller one—Franklin's—in his hands. Franklin turned and held out his arms behind him, as the aide worked the pack onto his shoulders.

"Thank you, Tchang. You're a good man to have along. How's our food holding up?"

Most of their supplies were stashed at the last camp. Three porters had stayed behind, warmly ensconced in their tents. This final run for the top was to be Franklin's, alone, and Tchang's, although he would get no credit. Only the expedition leader would go down in the record books, and that, only if he returned alive. Three men had lost their lives on this trek, two in the last year alone. Fools, Franklin had declared. A well-prepared mountaineer could commandeer any peak. It just remained to attack it with determination and a well-laid-out plan.

Today, he would be proved correct. Today, he would reach his goal.

"No one will starve," Tchang replied softly.

"No one? Those birds, what about them?" Franklin chuckled as he took his walking stick from Tchang. "I'm not sharing my next meal with them."

"No, sir. I wouldn't expect you'd want to."

The men started out. The summit was invisible, hidden by a ghostly hand. The eagles' cries were sometimes close by, and other times distant and forlorn. With the exertion, perspiration soon dampened exposed skin and hidden underlayers, and ice formed on furrowed brows. Clouds appeared with each breath, whipped away to become part of the ethereal fog.

They were men lost in their environment, with nothing before them and nothing behind. They had no place to go, and none to which to return. Each labored step was taken in a world of its own, and they began to struggle for breath.

"Hold," Franklin called out, as a black ghost flashed in front of his eyes. An eagle? Hardly, at this height. He wiped his glove across his face and felt ice crystals fall from his lashes.

"Sir?"

"I saw something. Listen for a moment." He held out his arm to forestall his aide's interruption. There it was, the crunching of snow in the silence.

Even the stream was frozen this high up. It was still snow, and it might or might not warm before winter claimed the mountain passes once again.

"Sir, we do not have time to waste." Tchang didn't make a move. Their pacing was Franklin's call.

"Quite right. We'll summit come hell or high water."

Around the next bend in the trail they found Franklin's black ghost. A whole convocation of birds danced in the snow, their wings held wide, their hooked bills open and exposing hungry mouths. It was as though they offered avian prayers for an upcoming meal.

"Tchang?" Franklin froze, and he turned to his aide. "What are they doing here?"

Tchang bowed his head respectfully, as though offering a prayer to the black creatures.

"It's as you say, sir. There is no life up here, and they do like live food."

Tchang turned to make his way back down the mountain as the buzzard-eagles overtook Franklin, ripping through his layers of clothing, and amidst his screams, began to feed.

Glitter

FOOTSTEPS CREAKED ON the treads of the stairs.

The bedroom door handle turned slowly. It protested with a squeak, and the handle paused; then it began to turn again, this time more carefully. With a click, the door released, revealing the light of a candle shining through.

"Lucy? Are you there?" A giggle of feverish anticipation accompanied the words.

The candle slipped through the opening, illuminating a thin figure dressed all in black, the color of midnight assignations. The build suggested a man. When he pushed his hood back, his smooth face suggested someone younger. He was decorated with color, glitter, and rhinestones, a character in a child's fantasy tale.

"Your mum's light was on. I was sure I'd get caught. I'm a day early for the wake."

The brightly festooned youth set the candle on a dresser cluttered with a young girl's dreams. It was a memorial of dried flowers, laughing pictures of friends, and scattered cosmetics of various colors and styles. Butterflies of plastic or silk, large and small, decorated the mirror. A hairbrush was littered with remnants of green and gold, two of the girl's latest experiments, both now history. The mirror on the wall reflected a covered form on the bed, the image dim in the flickering light, a girlish shape, underneath a neatly tucked sheet.

"I brought some soda like you like."

The boy sloughed off a pack, set it in a chair, and unfastened a long zipper that ran up one side and down the other. He pulled out two cans triumphantly and turned to the bed. He set one down on the dresser and popped the top of the other with a distinctive click. It began to foam, and he jumped backward, trying to drink the excess, as he searched for a waste bin. He stumbled into the door, kicked a metal can with his feet, and with a laugh, held the drink steady to let it bleed its excess life into the receptacle.

"Glad your mum didn't hear that." He grabbed the backpack and sat on the edge of the bed, taking another sip, before putting the can on the floor. "Want to see what else I brought? I told you I had one. Here it is."

Out of the pack, he pulled a clear jar with a brass screw-on lid. Inside, a butterfly of exquisite beauty flexed its wings. It seemed to glow in the dim light, with crystalline colors of red, gold, and azure. The boy held it close to his face, and his features lit up with multicolored light, reflected in his rhinestones and glitter makeup.

"Do you want to see? I'll show it to you. No one else knows about it. Lucy, you'll be the first."

He didn't look the bed's direction but put his hand on the lid and began to unscrew it. The butterfly quivered in anticipation, as if it knew it was about to be free. It crawled to the rim, and outside the glass, now it truly began to shine. The youth held out a finger, and the creature gently walked onto his skin. Each step it took left footprints of shining light and sparkling gemstones that only faded when it took to the air.

The youth's eyes followed it as it flitted around the room. It landed on the mirror, and soon, the plastic and silk butterflies seemed to take on a life of their own. Their wings twitched, and in minutes, living butterflies filled the air, the breath of their wingbeats brushing the candle flame into dancing shadows that sprinkled color across the walls.

He gave a small whistle, and the butterfly—the original one with the glowing wings—alighted on his outstretched finger. The rest gathered on his arms and head and shoulders.

"Lucy, it's time. You have to wake, now. My butterflies will show you how."

He walked gently to the bed, so as not to disturb the fluttering creatures, and he worked the taut bedding back. Underneath, Lucy's lifeless form lay with an empty expression and pale skin. She smelled of clean sheets and rosewater, a person whose life had only recently slipped away.

When he had her completely exposed, he held out his finger and let his butterfly alight on her chest, just over her heart. The glow of its wings increased, until Lucy's skin began to warm with a soft light. Soon, the form of the butterfly was sublimated into the brightness. The youth shook his arms and shoulders, driving the rest of the butterflies into the air. They began to settle on Lucy's limbs, face, and torso, until she was covered with their brightly colored wings.

The youth stepped away and retrieved his soda. His skin decorations sparkled in the changing light from the bed. He lifted his head to drink from the can, revealing a neck as colorful as his face.

When he heard a gasp of indrawn breath from the bed, he smiled. He set the can aside and retrieved the one he'd brought for Lucy. He found his way to the bed and knelt at her side. When she opened her eyes, he popped the top of the can and held it out to her.

"You're beautiful again, Lucy. Look in

the mirror and see."

Each butterfly had left a piece of itself where it had landed, and she sparkled in glitter and rhinestones. The most beautiful place was just over her heart, one that glowed in crystalline colors of red, gold, and azure.

The youth pulled one last item out of his pack. It was a black robe. Lucy slipped it on, and together, they fluttered out the door, their feet hardly touching the floor, leaving the candle to burn itself out.

Survivor List

ICY WIND SLASHED at the boy's face.

The rain danced its evil dance upon his head as he tried to get his bearings on the isolated beach. His life ring hung limply from one hand. The word *Britannic* wrapped around the side. He'd barely gotten out of steerage before the vessel had gone down. The explosion had shaken him to his core, and he could still barely hear.

"Hallo, is anyone there," he called. He couldn't tell if he yelled it or not, as he couldn't hear his own voice over the wind. He shivered violently, his wet clothes hanging limply on his thin frame. He'd been able to swim, the reason why he'd made it to shore. Others hadn't, especially those in his class. He'd seen the lifeboats going off, leaving dead bodies floating in the sea. He'd been desperate and had stripped his preserver from the shoulders of a dead man, badly burned and floating just where the ship had gone down. He'd watched the man sink, then he'd struck out for the distant shore, one arm in the ring, and the other paddling for all he was worth.

Now he wasn't sure he shouldn't have gone down with the ship. As his cold-induced convulsions grew more forceful, he dropped the ring at his side and trudged away from the water. The shore was rocky, and the climb was steep. In his mental fog, he tried to think where the ship had been. The Mediterranean, he thought. Near Greece, he expected. An island, certainly.

Voices caught his attention, and he surmounted the headland to find a group of men around a campfire.

"Hallo," he called once more. One of the men turned and waved him toward the flame.

"Come, boy! We've awaited your

presence. Warm your chilled skin."

"You could have answered," he bemoaned, as he drew close to the flames. "Anyone got any coffee?"

"Coffee. The boy wants coffee. What'll he be asking for next, a silk robe and a warm bath?" Laughter followed the words, and from more than one of the small throng.

"Just want to warm up," he offered. He had his hands out, wishing the flames were hotter. His chill must be worse than he thought.

"Might be difficult, at that. The warming up. Though, some claim they get more than they want. Their just desserts, so to speak." Another round of laughter, not quite as loud as the first.

"So, why didn't you answer? I called from the beach."

"T'weren't no call from the beach. Not that we could hear up here, anyways." An old man with ragged sleeves and fewer teeth than a newborn chicken cackled. "Bet it was raining down there, too."

The boy looked around, then up at the sky. The stars were out overhead, and the Milky

Way was visible just over the horizon. That was when he realized his clothes were dry, and the chill had faded from his limbs. The fire was no warmer, but he wasn't cold any longer.

"Thought it was." He shrugged. "Guess I was wrong. I was wet from my swim, and that was why I thought there was rain. Anyone can be a fool."

"So long's they don't stay a fool." A portly man smoking a pipe pulled it from his mouth to speak. As soon as he finished, he clamped his teeth back on the stem and drew in a deep draught, before letting it out again. A wreath of smoke encircled his head.

"We were near Greece, and I wonder if—"

"Still are," a voice interrupted. "Not that it's a Greece you'd recognize in your fondest dreams."

The boy couldn't see who spoke.

"Where at in Greece?" The boy had grandparents, and if they were close, he might make his way there.

"Kea, but it might be New Zealand, for all that it matters to you."

"I know Kea. I can get a boat—"

"No, you can't." Once again he was

interrupted.

"My grandparents live on Makronisos. They have a phone. I can call." He stood, now irritated with his rescuers. They hadn't actually rescued him, anyway. They hadn't warmed him at their fire, not really, and everything he said, they claimed the world was the opposite. "I'll find them on my own."

"Wouldn't do that, boy." It was the unseen voice, and now a man walked from the darkness, nattily dressed, in wingtips and a seersucker suit. He wore a jaunty hat angled to one side, and he held a long cigar in one hand.

"You can't stop me." The boy yelled the words, now angry beyond control. He could hear himself fine, which surprised him, just not enough to try to figure out why.

"Don't plan to. Still, I wouldn't do that, if I were you." The man took a puff of the cigar and held it inside for a too-long time, before letting it drift from his nose.

"I hate you. All of you." The boy took off for the shore, determined to find another way home. It was at the edge of the bluff that he drew to a startled stop. The rain pounded the beach, and far below, a boy lay on the sand, one arm in a life ring, with the waves washing over his legs.

"We tried to tell you, boy." An arm with a ragged sleeve wrapped his shoulders. "You ain't on the survivor list. You didn't make it, son."

Then the rain moved past the headland, and the remaining lifeboats could be seen making their way to shore.

All Hallows' Eve

DEATH LURKED IN every doorway.

Then, that was the curse of living in a funeral home. I'd grown up with it and thought nothing of seeing dead bodies on the way to breakfast, and new ones when I got off the bus after school.

Some of my friends thought it was creepy, but even more found it ghoulishly attractive. I always had requests for sleepovers on the weekends.

My sleepover friends were usually disappointed when my dad locked the doors to the funeral home before he went to bed. They wanted to explore the rooms of the deceased, prowl the dark corridors, and prod the stiffies.

I understood, having done just that over the years. After a couple dozen pokes at stiffened flesh, however, it becomes rote, just another porker to be dressed with flowers in a tiny room so the people they left behind could weep their tears of grief, then go back to their cubicles and earn their next paycheck.

They didn't have to live with death every day. I did, and I found it wasn't that big a deal.

At least when they didn't come back to life.

See, here's what you need to know about dead people. They aren't always *dead*. Don't be confused, here, because they *are* dead, but that doesn't mean they can't sit up and scare the bejesus out of you. I had that happen a time or two, and I swear, I messed my pants the first few times. Like, jumped-out-of-my-skin scared. The sort where you lay in bed the rest of the night quivering in fear, hoping the door doesn't open, because you just know the dead people are walking the hallways at night.

That's what my friends wanted to feel, so I understood. It's just that my dad feels respect for the dead. He thinks kids sneaking around in the darkness to get their jollies off the newly departed is inappropriate.

My dad needs to try being a kid, again. He needs to remember what it's like to lay in your bed and try not to wet yourself with the thought of dead people living under your roof. Well, not *living,* but you know what I mean.

That's why Jimmy and I came up with a plan.

To explain the plan, you have to know about dead people sitting up. See, the decomposition process produces gas inside the bodies. It expands, forcing the internal cavities to distort the body, sort of like a water hose when you first turn on the water. The hose bloats and uncurls, like it's alive, but it's not really.

That's what a dead person does sometimes. Not often, but occasionally. We planned to make sure it happened to my dad. In the middle of the night. When he least expected it.

And here's the good part. On Halloween. Friday. The start of the busy weekend.

The business side of the funeral home

closed early on All Hallows' Eve, as it always did, even though Friday nights were usually our busiest time. Dad didn't like to compete with the trick-or-treaters. He said Halloween was scary enough for children without having real dead bodies thrown in the mix. He didn't even work in the basement morgue, instead enjoying sitting out front handing out candy to anyone who dared open the gate to the scariest building in town.

My dad even put out decorations all over the front yard, just to join in the fun.

Now, I knew where Dad kept the keys to the morgue, and a fresh body had come in just that day. With Dad out front the entire evening, Jimmy and I had plenty of time to get things ready. Jimmy would lay out on the table, and I'd cover him with a sheet. Then I'd tell Dad I was hearing noises, and when he went to check, my friend would moan and sit up, giving my father a proper Halloween scare.

Perfect, huh?

It would have been, except for the storm that blew in about halfway through the evening.

Jimmy was already in place, and my dad called for me to hurry outside. The wind was scattering the decorations down the street, and I had to help retrieve them. Then the storm's second wave hit, with hail and lightning, and I was stuck for an hour on Mr. Robeson's porch in the next block.

By the time I got home, the stars had started to come out. Leaves and branches littered the sidewalks, with bright bits of color—candy wrappers and such—scattered in between. I was surprised to see the house fully lighted, like a holiday pumpkin, grinning drunkenly at passersby on the street. Then I saw the basement lights were on.

Jimmy! I'd missed the fun.

Then it hit me. I hadn't said anything to Dad about hearing a sound in the morgue. And he never went down there once he locked the door. Never. Not unless it was an emergency, and there hadn't been an emergency that I knew of. I mean, the storm, but nothing serious, nothing that would cause Dad to change his routine and head to the basement.

Then chills ran down my back when I

saw the flashing lights out back where the bodies were delivered. I tore through the front door and nearly ran into my dad.

"Whoa, Son. What's the rush?" He pulled off his glasses and slipped them in his shirt pocket.

"What are the lights for?" I panted as I looked at the door to the basement stairs. It was open wide.

"A misunderstanding, that's all. The body that was delivered today is involved in a police investigation, and they needed to retrieve it for autopsy. A mix-up, that's all. Nothing to worry about. I unlocked the basement and let them in. They're just leaving." Sure enough, a siren blipped, and through the back windows, I could see several cars pulling away from the house. "Come downstairs with me, and we'll lock up for the night." He disappeared through the door.

I sighed in relief. Maybe we could still pull this off. I hadn't seen Jimmy around, so he was probably still under his sheet. I started down the stairs after Dad.

"This is surprising!"

"What, Dad?" I was about to turn the corner into the morgue.

"The body's still here."

I stepped through to find my dad beside the covered form and scratching his head. I expected Jimmy to sit up at any time.

"The *dead* person?" I chuckled in anticipation, watching the sheet, waiting for it to move.

"Well, let's see what we have." Dad took the corner of the sheet and jerked it back, only it wasn't Jimmy lying there.

I never saw my friend again. He didn't show up at school the next week, and when I went by his house, there was a For Rent sign in the window. I don't know if the police autopsied the wrong person, or if Jimmy was so mad at me that he and his folks just left town.

I watch all the doors now. Dead people do that sometimes, just come back to life, especially if they're not really dead.

The Fairy Mask

My HAIR STOOD on end.

A shiver raced down my spine, and a lump came to my throat. It was him, wearing his clown suit, with its giant lapels, baggy pants, and outlandish tie. A sequined mask covered his eyes. Of course, he thought he was stylish, but foppish was the word. I'd never seen anyone so silly.

I stepped into the alley and reveled in the darkness, secure in the knowledge I hadn't been seen. The throng of partiers went by without me, the exuberant revelers in their flamboyant clothes setting off streamers of various colors and tooting horns as they passed.

How I wanted to be part of the crowd.

It wasn't to be. Wymann had made his decision, and now he had to live with it, no matter that he wanted me back. My goal was revenge, total and unmitigated revenge. I intended to get even in the cruelest way.

I was going to fall in love.

***

Once the street was clear, I darted into the empty expanse. The leavings of the Carousel Parade were everywhere, scattered bits of color, whiffs of heady cologne—or the scent of perfume—and there was nowhere the revelers hadn't been. Their detritus fluttered on the fire escapes, inside glass doors, and underneath the tramway rails. Here and there were discarded bottles, some with dregs unconsumed, and a few broken, warning stragglers to beware.

The cleaning crew would have it tidied up by sunrise, but for now, it was a wastrel scene of wild debauchery.

Just what I'd expect from Wymann's

posse.

Around the corner, the doors to a club were thrown wide, offering booze and a good time to everyone who dared. The sign above the door proclaimed *No Cover Charge*. That was enough for me. The people I saw entering were all costumed, so I knew what I wore wouldn't do. Street kids weren't allowed in, especially on Carousel Night, even if I used to be a regular in wealthier times. Opening my small pocket knife, I cut a strip from the bottom of my pale green shirt, and snipping two holes for my eyes, I tied it around my head. I shredded the loose ends and twisted them into windblown dreadlocks that bounced when I turned my head. Next, I shredded my pants from the knees down, twisting them to match. I worked on my sleeves to the same effect and kicked my shoes to the side. Now I was a dancing, barefoot pixie, and I would make magic for my drink.

I floated through the door, laughing and pretending pixie dust on everyone I met. Street clothes were strewn in a pile, removed to reveal the attendees' most outlandish costumes. I held out my hands to be kissed, and I giggled when people tried.

I kept my eyes moving, searching, not only for Wymann—there was nowhere else he could have gone—but more for someone to be my love. He had to be tall, handsome, and full of life. He had to make Wymann crazy jealous, so that he'd know I'm not a fool to be messed with twice.

Underneath the flashing lights, the dance floor throbbed. One man in a fairy suit caught my eye. He wore wings of diaphanous silk and a headpiece with glittering eyes. Not an inch of his skin could be seen. Everyone wanted to dance with him. Before long, I was caught up in the revelry, and I wanted to be his partner, too.

I set my plan into motion.

I moved onto the dance floor, flitting from partner to partner, never remaining too long. I only wanted the fairy man. I smiled and teased, flinging my arms in the air, always aware of my bare feet, and stepping lightly among the increasingly wasted crowd.

The fairy man proved hard to catch. Each time I pirouetted his way, his dance moves carried him another direction. I began to worry the sunrise would spoil my plan. I didn't wear a watch, and I'd long since been unable to afford a phone; but hours had surely passed, and desperation danced at my side.

Then he was there, tall like I liked, even more than Wymann, though that could have been the headpiece. I pushed another girl out of the way, pretending I could barely stand, and grabbed the fairy man's arm for support.

"Hi, there." I began to dance, setting my dreadlocks into motion.

"Hi-ya, back." He leaned in and whispered the words, his breath warm in my ear. His mask obscured his voice as it brushed my dreadlocks, and it seemed as sensuous as a lover's kiss.

"Are you new here? I haven't seen you before." I rippled my fingers and let them flow across his mask, smiling coquettishly underneath mine. He didn't answer, but I was certain I saw him smile beneath his sparkling disguise.

So we danced, for hours, it seemed.

Once, a drink found its way into my hand, and it was down and gone before I could blink. And another after that. Then the fairy man reached to a table, lifted a glass, and did the same. I had quit looking for Wymann. This had started out a game for me, a plan to make Wymann suffer, but it was becoming more.

I really was falling in love.

I no longer cared who was in the club, or who wasn't. If Wymann was watching, fine. If not, it was no skin off my back. I ached for a slow dance, where I could hold the fairy man in my arms. Why didn't they do slow dances, anymore? It was a mystery to me.

"Let's take a break." The fairy man leaned in, so warm, so familiar. It seemed I'd known him for a very long time. That's how I knew it was love. When it hits hard, you bond immediately, like you were meant to be.

"Sure." I fluttered my hands at faces I recognized, laughing and blowing kisses, but his hand on my shoulder kept pulling my thoughts back to him. Fairy man and me, we would be together forever. Love said so, and who can doubt the truth of love?

"Want to get out of here?" Fairy man had stopped beside the door.

"If you want." I was so heady in love that I didn't care what he asked. I'd do it just to be near him.

"Your shoes?" It was a good question. The pile of street clothes was higher than ever.

"Outside." I saw Wymann's foppish suit crumbled up in a corner. On impulse, I threw my arms around my fairy man and said, "I'm in love, and with you, forever and ever." I wondered if Wymann knew, although I could hardy care.

"I know." He laughed, so very like a laugh I knew.

"You!" I reached to his mask. "It can't be you." I twisted his mask from his head to find Wymann underneath.

I didn't care. I was in love, and we held hands as we wandered into the night.

Returning Home

THE GRAVESTONES STOOD row upon row.

They were soldiers, some long forgotten, and others freshly tended, dutiful sentries, each shouting its name.

Parker, Thomas Henry, *Corporal*

Lyon, Gilchrist James, *Private*

Stewart, George Cameron, *Flight Sergeant*

A scream shattered the silence, and then it was gone, no more than the sound of the wind pushing the evening fog across the green hills.

Inside the church, candles filled the window ledges, turning the stained-glass windows muddy with the growing darkness. They shut out the cries of the dead screaming from each and every stone.

From the raised dais at the front of the small sanctuary, a robed figure intoned a message to those gathered for the evening service.

"He must increase, but I must decrease. Our scripture is found in John 3:30."

The figure looked expectantly at the small crowd, glancing at each lined face. These were the survivors of those who rested in the yard. Mothers, fathers, wives, sisters, and grandfathers. Only the very young boasted unlined faces. Only they had escaped the tragedy of the war.

"These simple words of John the Baptist," the speaker went on, "whose feast we celebrate today, summarize the life of the Christian disciple . . ."

His words droned on, familiar ones listened to many times before. The devout—or desperate—followed his every word. Others, less filled with belief, watched the candles or the last of the light through the stained glass, as the evening faded to black.

"In all things, we want Jesus to

increase . . ."

The scream happened again, this time louder, and the speaker broke his rhythm. His face glistened, and after a moment, he started up again, repeating a few words. ". . . Jesus to increase, and our own will, our own desires, our own attachments, to decrease."

The sound of an aircraft in the distance, an old-fashioned prop-driven craft, made a loose pane of glass buzz. No one turned at the sound. Several people clasped their hands at their breasts, and one old woman, her scarf tied tightly under her chin, sobbed, with her hand over her mouth, as she fought vainly not to disturb the service.

Then there was a second plane, louder, and a third and a fourth. They buzzed the church, and in the distance, a bomb exploded. They were sounds that were heard a half-century before, and they were as fresh in the listeners' minds as if the day was yesterday.

It was the promise they'd waited on. It had been foretold by an old gypsy, to happen fifty years from the day when their sons and fathers and brothers had died.

They would return, if only the village had faith.

Then the bombs began to explode in earnest, one after the other, and the windows of the old building rattled like they would come out of their leaded frames. The speaker raised his voice to yell over the din, "In my heart, in my prayer, in my family, in my parish . . ."

At the word parish, noise exploded throughout the structure, the roof shuddered, and old dust began to rain through the air.

"Jimmy! It's my Jimmy out there!" It was the old woman with the scarf. She tried to stand, using her arthritis-crippled hands to pull herself from her bench.

"Hush, Maggie. Stay where you are." A man half her age patted her on the shoulder. "The time's not yet come."

Maggie sank back down, but tears streamed down her face, and she looked at the ceiling with unadulterated anticipation.

". . . in my study, in my leisure, in my entertainment—*may the Lord increase!*" The words thundered, yelled at the top of the speaker's voice.

At just that moment, all hell broke loose. The church windows shattered on one wall, and the strafing of machine gun fire chewed up the carved woodwork around the altar. One section of the roof, just over the chancel, exploded, then fell in slow motion, sending a shower of debris into the room.

The candles flickered, but none went out, even in the windows that were opened to the night sky. Flowers of explosions danced in the darkness, creating a garden of death.

It was a garden of delight to those in the church. It was a battle the oldest remembered, most had lived, and only the youngest found frightening.

Then men's voices could be heard outside the walls.

"Reload that gun, man!"

"Heads down! Incoming!"

"I've been hit! I've been hit!"

Then a scream like the one from before, except this time different. This was just outside, and it was a voice Maggie knew.

"It's my Jimmy. You all know my

Jimmy. That's his voice. It has to be."

As the back wall of the chapel crumpled under the onslaught, the attendees rushed into the aisles and toward the doors. They barreled into the scene outside, braving the battle, to search for the ones they loved. Thomas, Gilchrist, George, and Jimmy, too. They were all there, maimed, suffering, but whole and alive. All of them and more. Each name on each tombstone called out to its blood, and if blood was there, the man was found.

One by one the injured soldiers were brought into the ruined church. One by one, they were seated on the benches. Bandages and salve were pulled from bundles; coffee was poured from vacuum flasks; and sandwiches were offered to any who were hungry.

All the soldiers were hungry.

The men and their families huddled in the broken building as the battle raged around them. Though the night, they consoled one another, hugged warm flesh they thought lost forever, and thanked the Lord for their loved ones reunited.

When the sun arose the next morning,

the chapel was once more whole, seemingly rebuilt as it had been nearly fifty years before. The graveyard was different, though. All the graves except for one were overturned, the ground thrown aside, and the coffins empty.

Williams, John Cragg, *Lieutenant*. His young wife had died of a broken heart after the war, and there was no one to welcome him home.

His screams still rise above the old churchyard one lonely night each year.

The Hotel

IT WAS THERE, and then it was gone.

Why would a rabbit be on my bathroom floor? Of course, Miss Marjorie would have none of it.

"A rabbit on your bathroom floor? Oh, Mr. Sikes, you're pulling my leg again. I don't know what I'll do with the likes of you."

She sauntered off down the corridor laughing, her basket of washcloths under one arm, greeting the other guests as she checked in at each room. I gaped after her. The rabbit. *The rabbit,* I wanted to call after her.

I turned away, aware of the others who would hear.

Then Miss Marjorie would laugh, and the

others would laugh, and I'd never hear the end of it.

I didn't enjoy being the butt of practical jokes, or even jokes that were no more than misunderstandings. I had my standing within our small community, after all. I must maintain my dignity, at all costs.

I wondered if she would tell the Director. I hoped not, now that I thought about it. He might make a special visit to my room to see the rabbit, and if it wasn't there, what would he think?

He might rethink my residency permit. That wouldn't do. Few people qualified to live in such surroundings, with hired help, and linens changed daily—or weekly if the help were busy with other things. Still, they did get changed, and dusting got done from time to time. A little more often would be nice, but things were never *too* dusty.

Once, for a whole week, I got room service for all my meals. I wasn't sure why, except that I broke a plate during dinner, and Miss Marjorie had to clean it up. We usually make our way to the dining room—a grand space with a piano in one corner—where we can converse freely without fear of recompense. Once, I told a coarse joke, just among close friends, and the diners at my table laughed. It was retold during the evening, many times, I'm sure, because it came back to me through another resident, as if I'd never heard it at all.

I laughed and pretended it was brand new. Good manners, that's what that is.

One day, Miss Marjorie left me a whole stack of clean washcloths. I wasn't sure if she meant to, because I'd asked her in to check my bathroom drain, when the buzzer sounded. She set her basket down and hurried out the door, and she didn't return. That's when I decided she intended me to use them, and I did just that.

I scrubbed the toilet in my room, around the base, and inside, too. Then the window looked dingy by comparison, so I scrubbed and scrubbed. It was hard, because of the safety bars. The window wouldn't open very far, and I had to work my hand through to clean the other side. I did it, though, even if I left a little blood on the frame. I must have cleaned half the night, way past dark. I soon had a pile of soiled cloths filling Miss Marjorie's basket.

The next morning, Miss Marjorie seemed pleased to locate her basket. When she looked inside to discover the wadded and dirty cloths, she was less pleased.

"What have you been up to, Mr. Sikes? These look to be run over by a car." She shook one out, and sure enough, a black streak ran from one side to the next.

I pointed to my window, and she frowned, but I think she was pleased. No one had cleaned the windows recently, at least not since I've lived here.

Wanda in Room 302 threw a party the other day. She didn't have party favors or cake or anything. I don't know if that's allowed outside the dining room. There we can even sing and dance, if there's someone to play the piano, but in our rooms, when Miss Marjorie or the Director aren't around, we must have quiet parties, where we just sit and talk. Well, Wanda talked up a storm, telling how she's going to be like Rapunzel and let down her hair. I didn't know if she meant she has a boyfriend who might crawl up to her window, or she might climb down to run in the gardens without Miss Marjorie around. I didn't tell her about the blood on my window frame. If my arm barely fit, I didn't see how Wanda or her boyfriend would get through. I guessed she'd find out, and then she would know.

Today we have inspections. The staff does that sometimes. It's a good thing, too. We can't let the standards slip. Who knows who would be living in the next room, if we didn't take care of the small infractions before they got out of hand? Sneak a slice of bread from the kitchen, let a few crumbs fall behind your bed, and the mice will find you. That's for certain. They can smell food a mile away.

Speaking of mice, this morning I found a hole in the sleeve of my dinner jacket. I was certain it was chewed by a mouse. I thought of Wanda and her long hair. I wondered if she'd brought in a nest of mice in her tresses the last time she strolled the grounds. I almost spoke to Miss Marjorie about it, but I remembered her frown when I cleaned the windows with her cloths, and I didn't want to get Wanda in trouble. I decided I could live with the hole in my sleeve.

We have an outing planned. We get to ride on the community bus. I wonder if the windows have been cleaned. The bus windows have bars, too, and that's probably why they don't get wiped down. I guess it would take a long time. I wouldn't mind, if I could borrow some of Miss Marjorie's cloths. It was hard to see out on our last trip, and I like to enjoy the view.

We get a piece of candy after we ride the bus, but only if we're good. We get to go to the spa. We get our teeth looked at, needles poked in our arms, and someone taps our backs to make sure we're really healthy. One time they combed my hair over and over, telling me all my little friends had to find another home. I laughed at that. I didn't know my friends could live in my hair.

I like to suck on my candy on the way back from the spa. I hold it in my cheek, and sometimes I make sucking noises. I don't bite it, though, not very often, and never before we drive through the big gate. I like the big gate. Right beside it is a fancy sign with words I can't read. I know my letters, but one word is too big for me to understand.

S. A. N. I. T. O. R. I. U. M.

I guess that's a word for a fancy hotel.

I like where I live.

House for Sale

THE LONG HOURS of my job were taking a toll.

I guess I'd overslept. It wasn't like me, as I'm usually up at first light no matter how late I work. When I turned the bedroom blinds, the morning sun nearly blinded me.

Then, maybe it made sense. The blinds had been closed, the alarm clock was blank, and the light switch didn't illuminate anything. The power was probably out. Just as well. My eyes burned with what was likely a sleep-deprived hangover, and I appreciated the dark.

I closed the blinds and turned away. Bleary-eyed, I headed downstairs for breakfast. I could still have sweet rolls, even without power. Or eggs. The gas would still be on, and I could heat coffee the old-fashioned way, if I could find my dad's old stovetop percolator. If it wasn't in the pantry, it'd be with the camping gear.

I didn't pay much attention to the blank walls as I passed the stair landing. The absent console with its usual spray of flowers formed a chasm of empty space. Even the missing greenery along the banister failed to get my attention.

Stepping into the den was my wakeup call. The house was empty.

Even the furniture had gone AWOL.

"Cindy?" My wife, short for Cynthia. "Cindy, what's going on?"

We weren't redecorating, not that I knew. I glanced through the front windows—at least we still had the draperies that had come with the house—to see the familiar landscaping I'd trimmed over the week-end. The flowers that had attracted us to the property when we'd moved in bordered the drive. We'd replanted them every year. They were blooming profusely, so I had to be in the right house. I ran my hands over the wall where the sofa had been the night before, searching to find the holes in the wall telling of the pictures that had been there.

I was hoping I wasn't crazy.

"Jamie?" My seventeen-year-old, Jameson. A pain in the neck, sometimes, like I was at that age. We'd moved in when he was four. He should be at school. Still, with today, who knew? Maybe he was on the remodeling team that had carted the furniture away.

I called for Kimmie, my daughter. She was barely walking when we first toured the property. She was the reason we bought it. She claimed her bedroom with a screech of delight, and it was a done deal from that point on. At fourteen, she was the least likely to go off the radar. She was my peacemaker, the one who tried to get everyone to get along.

Sometimes it worked. Sometimes it didn't. I didn't know which category an empty house fell into. Cindy and I hadn't had any arguments, any serious ones, anyway, not lately, and she'd even taken to kissing me as I left for work.

Well, not today. I hadn't made it to work. I wondered if my car was in the garage.

It wasn't, and I couldn't even find a phone to call my boss. Cindy—if she'd moved out and left me like I suspected—had even taken those. Every one, even the one in my office.

My office's empty bookshelves surprised me. I kept very little fiction in the house. Mostly my books were job related, law books and such. I know you can now look up everything on the computer, but computers go down, don't they? And sometimes the internet connection just isn't there. I like backup copies I can access at any time.

I heard the front door, a key jiggling in the lock. I lifted one of the slats on the wooden blinds—I can just see a portion of the porch from my office—to discover a couple. I couldn't make out their faces, but she seemed to be holding the hand of a toddler. A nicely coiffed female was facing me, and she gave a professional smile before withdrawing a key and pushing the door wide.

I was flabbergasted. How did this

woman have a key to my house? We'd lived here thirteen years. The Kelbys across the street had a key, for emergencies, you understand, and for when we were out of town, but no one else. Cindy's parents lived in Chicago, and mine in Fort Lauderdale. Even they didn't have keys.

I wasn't dressed to greet anyone, so I surreptitiously followed them as discreetly as possible, trying to make sense of things. I couldn't catch everything they said, but I managed to get the gist of the conversation pretty well.

"Notice the large kitchen. You'll see all new countertops, and the refrigerator stays with the house."

A realtor? I might have known when I saw her on the porch. I recognized her face, now, from signs around the neighborhood.

The young couple made a noncommittal sound, and the realtor let out a light laugh.

"You say you have a son? At four, he must be in preschool today. You say his name is Jameson?"

That caught my attention. Another mumble from the couple, then a laugh from the realtor.

"Jamie. I'm sorry. I should have remembered. Your daughter might want this room for her bedroom."

The voices were growing fainter, and I moved into the kitchen as they made their way toward the downstairs bedrooms. I caught up with them as they disappeared into my daughter's room, and the little girl let out a high-pitched squeal. My eyes opened wide with surprise.

"Sold," I heard my voice from the other room. "Kimmie loves it. We don't need to see any more houses."

I knew I didn't have to worry any longer. The furniture would be delivered in two weeks. Until then, I had the house to myself, a vacation of sorts. I wouldn't even need to go to work.

I headed back upstairs to bed. I found I liked sleeping in, at least when I was the only one home.

Wedding Vows

THE LIGHTS FLICKERED and then went off.

Then the sirens started. An earthquake was coming, and we knew it wouldn't be the last time.

"Grab what you can," I yelled. "Hold on until it's over."

Me? I went for the Steuben crystal vase on its display stand. I saw the other patrons in the shop dropping purses and bags, doing their part to mitigate the damage. Two stalwart men gripped the sides of a glass cabinet, so it didn't crash to the floor. One woman put her back to an antique grandfather clock, just as the chimes started to ring.

The people outside the shop were like crazy ants in the face of a storm, and then, the shaking started.

Every time, I ask myself why I haven't quake-proofed my shop. I curse my laziness and vow to invest whatever it takes to ensure my goods are safe and sound.

Here's the catch. It's not the quakes.

Rather, it's that they aren't quakes.

Nope, we're not having earthquakes, not here in Salt Lake City. We've got a whole different sort of problem going on.

Now, I'm not a believer, not in Mormonism, but I can live and let live just fine. If the people who make up this fine city want to live according to their religion, multiple wives and all, then I've no problem with that. More wedding gifts, is what I say, and that drives my business.

There's only one problem. I'm not sure God agrees with my line of thinking.

Now, don't be imagining that God's got anything against me. These quakes are happening to everyone, right across the state, but mostly here in the city. Everyone's affected. How do I know it's God?

The angels.

You heard that right. The angels. Not the sports team, but real, winged angels, the sort that fly around in the sky and make you want to give up on going out during the day.

'Cept that night is no better.

In the daytime they carry trumpets. It's the noise that makes the quakes. They all raise them to their lips in unison, and when they blast away, the whole city begins to shake.

That's why we get siren warnings now. The city fathers have installed watch towers, and when the angels gather, and the horns are about to blow, the watchers set off the sirens, and the city hunkers down until the quakes are over.

Nighttime is worse.

That's when the angels come out with flaming torches. Sometimes the flames break off and fall to the ground, and buildings ignite. Last month, a whole block went up over on Lehman, taking out seventeen houses and half of Fairbourne Station, with only dust and blackened rubble left.

Since then, no more nighttime weddings, if you've already got a bride. The first wedding doesn't seem to count. That's okay with the angels. It's the second that brings them on, with their trumpets and torches of fire.

As near as anyone can tell, nothing else happens afterward. It's not like the guilty parties get roasted over open flames or anything. They just get an earth-shaking trumpet blast when they say their "I do's", or a flaming blast of fire, if it's nighttime. Then they're left alone.

The city fathers have banned nighttime weddings, now. If you want a second bride, or a third or a fourth, you have to plan it in the daytime. You know, before God and everyone, so to speak. Some people have complained, not liking being forced to take off work just to get married, but hey, it's better than burning half the city down.

Of course, the true believers totally dismiss this line of thinking. To them, the angels are a celebration of joy. They even explain why none show up for a man's first marriage. He hasn't fulfilled

God's instruction to be fruitful and multiply. One bride's not enough. It's only on the second that the angelic hoards get excited and come to earth to blast their horns.

Or roast their earthly supplicants to death. Whichever.

There've been protests organized to settle the matter. A few bottles were thrown, some overly ripe tomatoes. The city's marriage license division on South State got fire-bombed, but no one was seriously hurt. Not any worse than the angels have done, anyway, and it was in the daytime, so it was dismissed as an accidental fire.

At least no one died, like in the Lehmen Avenue inferno. That one burned for three days, and two firefighters succumbed from smoke inhalation. What a way to go!

Not one wants to admit that there might be a way to make the angels go away. Just close the marriage license division. Go ahead and live together. Whatever. The angels don't care about that. Co-habitation isn't their thing. They just don't want the people of this good city to make it official.

Me? I'm torn two ways. I want to save my shop, which means the angels need to go away. I also want to save my business, which means I want as many people to have weddings as possible.

I did buy an atlas the other day. I've been searching for a new place to live, one where they don't have weddings at all. In the Trobriand Islands, there's no traditional marriage ceremony, and that means no angels.

Now I'm in the market for a suitcase. Anyone got an extra one for sale?

The Last Birthday

THE DAY WAS my 940th celebration of life.

My birthday, that is. It would be my last.

By some measures, I was only 28. I really was, if you want to look at it from my viewpoint, because each time I returned to earth, twenty years had passed.

Now, everyone I knew when growing up is dead, unless they were also on the Intergalactic Force. It was our bane, to leave everyone behind, and to have them age away from us.

I was eighteen on my first trip. My girl—since we were fifteen—was excited to see me in my new uniform. Of course, I was just a private, but the uniform was a smancy one, with braid and a gold logo on the front that showed a solar system out in the far reaches of the galaxy. Me? I expected the logo was something stylized just because it was beautiful. I kissed her hard the day I left. I was just gone three weeks, not thinking she would be nearly forty when I returned.

I shouldn't have been surprised. I guess I was all caught up in the starry-eyed side of things, and it was there in the contract. A warning in big, red print. That's youth, though. Never thinking things through. I never did run into her, like she'd vanished from the face of the earth.

I guess she was pretty upset when I didn't return.

I had a month on earth that time. You'd be surprised how many girls want to be with a Force guy. To them, I was a twenty-year veteran. They had no clue I'd been on the job just three weeks. I was hardly experienced, still green behind the ears. I knew space terminology, though, enough to impress them, and I had been given a new uniform. They'd redesigned them in the years we were gone.

Two weeks in I met a girl I really liked, and we took a room together. It was like a honeymoon. We slept late, she made me breakfast in bed, and in the afternoon, we fed the ducks in the park.

I guess she didn't think about the time thing, or she didn't care. When I got up that last morning and put on my uniform, she kissed me like I was off to work and would be returning for supper.

I looked for her at the launch, but of course she wasn't there. The guys and I cracked jokes about the girlfriends we were leaving behind, and I let it go. I was still eighteen, and I was heading out to the stars for three weeks with my buddies.

The second time in, my dad had passed. I felt bad I hadn't gotten in to see him last time, but it had only been three weeks since I'd been home, and besides, I was with my girl. I'd phoned but never thought about flying up to Des Moines for a visit. I did get up to see Mom that layover. It was hitting me that I wouldn't get another chance.

My third time in, I ran into a cutie that reminded me of my teenage sweetheart. We spent an evening over dinner, and I told her of the planets we'd visited across the vast cosmos: Galitron, with its sugar-sand waterfalls, Balitore, overflowing with diamond seas, and more, so much more.

I had a hard time leaving that trip. On the last night, she told me I might know her grandmother. Yeah, I discovered. I did. I had left her behind sixty years before.

I was still eighteen, and I would be for another three trips. It seemed the world was moving on without me. I determined I wouldn't get attached to anyone, ever again. I would become a playboy, out with a different girl every night, not caring who I left behind.

Over the next three trips, I began to accumulate quite an entourage. I knew I'd been careless as my nineteenth birthday approached, and I'd left behind a few young'uns. More than a few, actually. Thirty-seven beautiful women, with thirty-seven sons and daughters, all of them older than me, and that was just from my first wild foray into the wiles of wanton womanizing.

By the third trip, I had great-grandsons

lining up to shake my hand and have their picture taken with me.

All that slowed down a bit eventually. I never knew if the beautiful dame who was hitting on me in the bar might be a descendant of mine. I was relieved when the IF came out with a test for that. Just swab her skin with a special tab, and my phone could tell me if she was a genetic match or not.

It started getting difficult finding a partner that wasn't a family relation. By the time I was twenty, I was forced to travel to the moon to find a woman where I hadn't fathered at least one of her parents or grandparents somewhere down the line.

By twenty-one, Mars was my only option. Heck, I even had a great-great grandson on our ship one trip, and he was older than me. That'll shake the years out of your socks, if anything will. We hit it off pretty well, though, and I was glad to spend the three weeks alongside someone with whom I had so much in common.

I did warn him away from going out again. I don't know if he listened. He wasn't on my ship at the next launch, and, of course, by the time I returned, he could have been twenty years older, or on a run to Deneb, his timeframe completely skewed from mine.

When I hit twenty-five, I knew there was a problem I wasn't going to be able to get around. Every girl I swabbed turned up with my DNA. It didn't matter the color of her skin or her ethnic background, they were my daughters. From Mars to Europa, my genetic material had infiltrated them all. The head of the space agency laughed off my concerns, telling me they were like third cousins, and where he was from, third cousins were marrying material.

I had no illusions that I would be alone the rest of my life. I had lived a life of luxury and ease—if mostly onboard my ship—and I had thoroughly messed up any chance that I might one day fall in love and settle down. I didn't want to ply the stars forever, while the earth grew old and crumbled around me. I wanted to go off to a little place with a woman I could love, and live out my years gardening, fishing, or something.

It didn't look like I had a choice in the

matter.

Then, one day, our ship arrived just as a fellow ship set down on the tarmac. I got to talking to several of the crew to find out they had been out nearly as long as me. One of the girls looked very familiar, and gosh darn, if my old girlfriend hadn't gone and signed up with the IF two years after I left on my first run. With the overlapping schedules, she was now twenty-six to my twenty-eight, and that was about perfect in my book.

The years have flown, and I got to thinking the other day, I haven't caught a pike in nearly four months. I might need to head out to the river, just as soon as I get the back forty plowed.

Of course, by now, my hands are weathered, and age-spots decorate them like a leopard's paws. I quit having birthdays after my last intergalactic run, because I don't care. I've got a girl, and she loves me like I am.

The Rock

THREE OF US, the only ones left.

We were the only ones to make it to the island.

For days, the bodies washed up on the shore, one after another. Even more, probably, were carried away again before we found them. We'd never know, since we weren't allowed to fraternize and hadn't learned anyone by face or name. We were kept locked in the hold, not even allowed the sight of the sky, as we battled the wind and the rain that finally took the ship down.

We were Frenki "The Arm" Edelstein, known for his kills with his hands, alone; Sammie

"Shameless" Giancola, often called The Rifleman, because the longer the gun, the more likely you were to die; and me, Rodrigo "Righteous" Duterte, because I never disclaimed a robbery or a murder. To do so was to lose my self-respect.

We were free, but we weren't freed. We were bound in shackles, and the iron had begun to rust. If the rust worked into our skin, it would kill us just as surely as the men who washed up on the beach.

I called to The Arm, "Hey, man, bring me a bigger rock."

I'd been pounding for hours, and I had the manacle bent, but it wouldn't break. I wanted to be truly free, from this metal, from this island, and from other men telling me what to do.

"Get your own, Diego—" The name was a slur, intended to rile me, but I let it go. "—I'm busy with my own rock." He held one in his hand, black and veined with gold, and he grinned as he smashed it against his leg irons. His calf jumped with the impact, and he raised it and smashed it again.

"Rifleman," I hollered. He was off to

himself, lying on a flat rock, and letting the surf wash over his legs. It washed over his manacles, too.

"Yeah?" He raised up on his elbows and looked at me sleepily. That was a disguise. The Rifleman was never sleepy. It was one of his deceptions. Make people careless around you, and that gives you the opportunity to strike.

"I need a bigger rock." I held up the one I'd been pounding with to show him how small it was.

I felt it was fair. At one point, we'd been chained together, arm to arm. We'd sailed away from Devil's Island, supposedly inescapable, a hellhole of a rock that had been made into a prison. On the rock, they didn't bother with chains or bars. The sea was your prison. It locked you in as good as iron ever did.

The chains had gone on when the three of us were transferred to the mainland. We'd been in the storm for days, driven to who knew where, and then the ship had gone down. It was a blessing from God, releasing us from our earthly penance, and giving us a chance to start again.

If we could get the iron smashed away.

Our first attempts had been on the chains at our wrists. The chains had broken free at the others' arms, but I still wore them on mine. They were heavy, and it made it difficult to move about easily. I had helped free them, and it was their duty to aid me.

They seemed not to think so.

I tossed my rock the Rifleman's direction. "You're doing nothing, man. Bring me a bigger rock, and we'll work on your iron together."

He looked at me with hooded eyes. "Will do neither me nor you any good. My manacles will rust away some day, and then I'll be free."

"Ache," I moaned, standing and lifting my chains as I began a search for a larger stone, but not too large, as I still had to be able to lift it. The sun pounded my back. When we first washed ashore, we had shivered with the cold. Now, what I wouldn't give to have the sea wash over me again. I would, however, sink to the bottom with the chains I carried.

It was unfair for me to be so burdened.

And I was sweat-encrusted, my bowels needed to move, and hunger was a fist in my gut. I looked at the sky overhead. At least we were free. I hefted the chains attached to my arms. Well, freer than I had been three days before.

By evening, I had one leg freed, and the other was nearly busted loose. I had to be careful. The metal was beginning to rust, and in the smashing, I had bent it until it had begun to pinch my skin. Infection was a constant worry, and I prayed for the metal to give way soon.

"Success is mine!" The Arm leaped to his feet, tossing his rock aside. He couldn't even toss it my direction. He still wore his iron bracelets, but his ankles were bound no longer. He danced in the sand, calling out, "Freedom shall be mine!"

I crawled toward his rock, dragging my chains. If I pounded the night through, I could surely be out of my prison iron. The Rifleman continued his siesta on the shore, even if he had moved up the beach to a new rock. The water still lapped at his feet.

By the light of a small fire, and with aching arms and a sore back, I released my final irons late into the

night. Tomorrow. In the morning, at first

light, I would construct a raft and make my way to sea. My two companions? I didn't care any longer. They had refused to help me, and I would abandon them without a care. They were as useless waste to me, less than worthless. I would be glad to be rid of them. I relaxed onto the shore and fell into a deep sleep.

I awoke to the sun and several troops, one in a French captain's uniform, coming over the ridge. In my bleariness, I called to them, "Where are we? Our ship sank offshore, and we need rescue."

"Rescue?" The captain laughed. "You're on Devil's Island, right where you belong."

I was immediately in despair. We'd sailed for days, and instead of finding hope, we'd become shipwrecked back where we started. I looked at the rock which I'd used far into the night.

The Rifleman had been right. Removing my iron had done me no good at all.

The Transfer

"WHAT HAVE you done?" the headmaster said.

All eyes now turned to me as he stood over the lifeless body on the playground. Five electrical burns were spaced over the pale face, in the shape of the fingertips on a boy's hand.

I blinked twice before I realized what must have occurred, but it couldn't be undone, even if I hadn't followed procedure. The school nurse should have monitored the entire process. I tried to remember exactly how it had happened, but it was a blank in the final moments.

Then, it would be. How could I

remember what my other self had done?

You see, I attend a school for the terminally ill. No one lives if they are assigned to Englemont Prep, not for long, anyway. And attendance is compulsory. No child is exempt, once they've received a terminal diagnosis.

I received mine at thirteen. I kept getting headaches, especially anytime I bumped my head, and I learned my brain was filled with unruptured aneurysms. Each one was potentially fatal, and they were swelling exponentially.

It was only a matter of time.

My head was going to go, and I got an immediate placement at Englemont. It was a lucky day for me, because under any other circumstances, I'd be dead already.

Well, I am, but not now. One me is dead, but the me I am now is in trouble for not following procedure.

Nurse Wilkins was going to be so angry.

"Come with me, Torrance Philby." The headmaster took me by the arm, and with a firm step, we made our way toward the building.

Torrey. I go by Torrey. Why does he always get it wrong?

Pairs of identical eyes watched us, the twin faces of each of my classmates. They knew this could happen to them as easily as it had happened to me. Most of them would have more warning of the impending transfer: respiratory distress syndrome, diphtheria, meconium aspiration syndrome. The causes were endless. Cancer, even. Why couldn't I have succumbed to neuroblastoma or leukemia?

No, I got hit with deadly aneurysms that could take me out at any time—and without warning!

My only option had been to remain bedfast, with my twin at my side, waiting patiently for one of my aneurysms to burst, for my deadly fate to come upon me. Still, I could have lived for years with nothing more than regular headaches, and who wanted to be in a hospital bed that long?

I took my chances, forged my medical report, and said the things in my head had stabilized. They hadn't, but it got me outside to play with the other kids.

Now I was in trouble for certain.

Death at Englemont was a hushed affair. We only learned someone had "crossed over" when they checked out of school and made their way back into normal society. An empty dorm room; a desk awaiting a new student; occasionally a farewell party, if the student had been at Englemont several semesters. Most of us didn't stay that long, given barely time enough to get acquainted with the staff.

Remember, we were terminally ill before we got our campus assignment. We were ready to go. We came knowing it was a matter of time. We were only here to ensure our twin lived to make his or her way back into the world to enjoy a long and productive life.

The disappointing thing as the headmaster led me from the playground was the lack of interest in the dead body. It no longer felt like mine. Still, it seemed rather forlorn, abandoned, a husk of life that was no longer interesting to the rest of the students.

Or to the headmaster.

After a brisk walk through the hallways, with our heels sounding bright on the marble floors, we turned into the nurse's office. She glanced up from her paperwork at her desk and looked me over, immediately understanding what had happened.

How can nurses always see these things? We were twins. How could she know I was this Torrey and not the other one? It must be in our faces, the way parents can always tell their identical children apart. Intuition, perhaps, or an understanding of what makes us tick. Maybe our expressions, I didn't know.

"Torrey, let me see your hand." Nurse Wilkins stood and walked my direction. She paused at the headmaster's side and said quietly, "Mr. Unger, you may go. I can handle this. If the body hasn't been removed, do so now."

"Right, right," he said, clearing his throat. "I'll get right to it." He turned and was gone out the door.

"Your hand, Torrey?"

I held it out, and she inspected my fingertips. Sure enough, each finger was blackened where I'd placed my hand on the dead boy's face to complete the transfer.

"I suppose you fudged the medical forms for more time on the playground. Is that so?" She looked at me over the tops of her reading glasses. Her eyes didn't criticize me, as though she understood.

I nodded my head.

"Well, this hand needs replaced. Hold here." She rubbed the scarred fingertips, and after a few moments turned and opened a cabinet. She searched for my name, then pulled out a hand that exactly matched mine. The base had a dongle that would connect to my arm for full functionality. "Roll up your sleeve, and hurry up, now. I've got work to do, and this isn't it."

She took my arm and twisted my hand hard, until it snapped free. She unplugged and tossed the old one in the garbage, then set the new one in place and plugged it in. With a stroke of her thumb, the skin merged over the seam. I wriggled my fingers.

"Now that you've transferred to your mechanical clone, you'll have a good life, Torrey. I'll phone your parents and let them know you're ready to go home."

"I'm not in trouble?" That was my prime concern.

"No, Torrey. Your clone did the right thing, transferring you over as soon as your body began to die. That was a very good thing."

I grinned and hit myself on the side of my head just for fun. No headache.

I hoped my parents hurried up. I was ready to go.

Disneyland

DAD JUST SAT and cried.

He cried for three whole days. His face was blotchy, and his eyes were red. Then one day he just stopped, wiped his face, and said, "Let's go to Disneyland."

We whooped and danced around. Disneyland!

It wasn't like we hadn't been before, but we hadn't been since *that*. You know, the *thing* that happened.

The one no one wants to talk about.

This was like a return to before, and we couldn't wait to get going.

Of course, it wouldn't be easy like

before. We had to scrounge around for gas for the car. Mrs. Belkin had a little bit in her lawnmower, and she assured us she wasn't mowing anymore. We might as well use it up, so we siphoned it out. It was only about a gallon, but that would get us part of the way there.

Mr. Lowe had a reserve tank on his generator. He threatened us if we touched it, but it was Disneyland. How could we not? So Zach—he's my oldest brother—clambered over his fence and got nearly three gallons. That was a prize worth just about anything. The good part? Mr. Lowe wouldn't notice until after we were gone, so we didn't particularly care. He could do his worst, but we would have Disneyland to remember.

I'm not sure where the five-gallon can came from, but it was full when Dad showed up after disappearing for most of Saturday morning. Zach started to ask, and Dad just shook his finger and used a funnel to pour it into the car. He gave the empty can to Zach and told him to hide it in the woods.

I kinda felt guilty, like we were doing something wrong, but it was Disneyland! I couldn't stay guilty for long. We would have so much fun!

We raided the canned goods in the basement to take with us. Pork and beans were okay even cold, so that was good. We packed the last two cans of tuna, and at the back of one bin, I discovered some Vienna sausages we'd overlooked. It's good Dad got to the store before all the shelves were emptied. They haven't restocked in a long time, and Zach says he's not sure they ever will.

We're hoping Willie—my middle brother—gets home in time for the trip. He's on a hunt with a friend of his, eager to get a deer. We could eat for a week on a big one, but we don't know how long they'll be gone. He learned there was a herd east of Sacramento, and that's way north of here. We'll leave him a note in case he returns while we're gone.

Dad says we can't take many toys or games with us, because we'll be shopping along the way. Some grocery stores might still have inventory, and if we locate one, we'll cart away as much as the car will hold. Dad says he's glad Mom wanted a station wagon. She was smarter than he knew, even if the *thing* caught her as much by surprise as it did everyone else.

Now, if all this is sounding like the end of the world, it's not. No way. See, we don't have to go to school any longer. Dad insisted we bring our books home, and he tells us we must study for at least an hour a day, but I tossed my math book away before I got home, and no one has said anything. Also, we no longer have to mow the yard. The grass is nearly knee high, and it's soft to roll around in. When Bradly and I play hide-n-seek, I lay down in the yard, and he sometimes can't find me. Bradly's my littlest brother, by the way. He's only four.

When we pulled out of the drive, Dad left the garage door open just a bit. The curtains, too, so people would think we were still at home. Mrs. Belkin knows we're gone, but no one else. Zach says it's better that way, and he should know. He was in college before the *thing,* and he learned a lot of stuff there.

I don't know why we left in the middle of the night, though, and Dad didn't turn the lights on. There are broken cars all over the street, and I had to cover my eyes, 'cause I didn't want to see if we hit one.

We didn't find any stores still stocked. Dad drove into Bakersfield and Palmdale and checked several stores, but they were bare. Zach suggested smaller towns, as they had fewer people to empty the shelves. Dad agreed that we would stop looking until after we visited Disneyland. I think the gas gauge had something to do with their decision. When Zach drove, he would sometimes tap the gauge. I think he hoped it would change, but it never did.

Disneyland wasn't as much fun as I remembered. Mickey wasn't there, and none of the rides were working. We sat in the train cars on the railroad and pretended it carried us around the park. There wasn't any water in the canal boats, but it was fun to pretend. Space Mountain was scary, and Bradly cried, so we didn't go inside. The best was the Indiana Jones Adventure. We climbed the pyramid and could see all across the park.

Somewhere, Zach found some gasoline in a backup generator. He used a bucket to ferry it to the car, and now we have a full tank. Dad says we're going to Mexico. We can live on the beach and fish in the sea. I asked about Willie, and Zack shushed me, telling me Dad left him a note, and he'd find us if he could.

Now I'm in the back playing with Bradly. I found a Mickey Mouse cap in a busted-up gift shop, and he laughs when I put it on.

I'm glad we went to Disneyland.

I wonder if Mexico will have a Ferris wheel.

The Sheriff

THE ALARM CLOCK rang.

I glanced to the bedside table. It was 74 minutes past 18. I did a double-take, sitting up and grabbing the unusual clock. I shook it, reading the numbers again.

18:74. What time was that? This was my morning to sleep in.

I yawned and shrugged. Whatever, it was time to get up. I threw the blankets back and swung my legs over the edge of the bed. I was surprised when my feet touched rough floorboards instead of my plush wall-to-wall. The unexpected sensation made me take stock of my room. My 55-inch television. It was gone. Stolen? I didn't know. My heart pounding, I stood and bumped my head. As I rubbed my newly wounded scalp, I cursed the rough, hand-hewn beam that crossed my ceiling. It hadn't been there the night before.

Had someone redecorated during the middle of the night? Not likely. It was more probable that I had been absconded with by mysterious vigilantes and secreted to a place of unknown locations until my ransom could be obtained.

Unknown to me, at least. I had no idea where I was.

I moved to a shuttered window and unlatched two coarsely sawn boards. The iron s-hook make me smile. It could have been made in a blacksmith's shop. Not with care, either, as though the utility of its manufacture was its driving purpose, not beauty or esthetics.

The glass was thick and wavy—hard to see through—but outside was no city street I'd ever seen. Was that a . . . it was! A horse-drawn buggy, and it was loaded with crates and coarse sacks of *something*.

The driver raised a whip and let it snap,

and the animal at the forefront jerked ahead, setting the wheeled conveyance into motion.

As the contraption moved out of sight, I noticed what its movement had left exposed. A water trough.

A water trough? On the city street?

This place wasn't a real city, though, was it? Not like the New York I lived in. Where were the office towers, the honking taxis, and the teeming throngs? This street was virtually desolate, with only a handful of people wandering its sidewalks. A woman in an ankle-length dress carrying a parasol, with a man beside her in a black, stovepipe hat, sauntered along.

I turned and leaned my back against the wall, my heart pounding. A movie set. That had to be it. I had been transported to Hollywood. It explained every-thing, well, except for how they got me all the way across the country. It seems I would remember that.

Where were the cameras? I glanced outside again, searching, but found nothing. Spying a suit of clothes draped across a simple chair, I lifted them and frowned. Era-specific, if this movie was set in the time I suspected. They seemed my size, and I pulled them on. At the bottom of the pile was a gun in a belted holster, with a metal star etched with the word Sheriff.

"Oh!" I smiled, now getting into the mood. "I play the important role. Bad guys, here I come."

I clipped the weapon around my waist and attached the star to my shirt. The boots seemed crudely constructed, unlike the city shoes I was used to wearing, but they fit well enough. I found a western hat on a bureau, and I slipped it on. Stepping out of my room, the boots had me rocking from side to side, with a swagger that was amusing. I looked and the soles were worn on one side, suggesting that someone bowlegged had worn them frequently. Outside, I was greeted by a well-dressed man I didn't know.

"Sheriff, good morning." He tipped his hat with a smile.

"And to you." I had decided to play my part, and I did so with gusto. I searched for the cameras along the tops of the buildings and inside the windows. They were well hidden, if they were there.

"Mommy, it's the sheriff." A child's

voice filtered from across the street. She ducked behind her mother's dress.

The city was eerily silent, and I could hear every word. It dawned on me that there were no air conditioners running, no chugging diesel engines from city buses, and no ringing cell phones.

The mother shushed her child, saying more softly, "Hush, Rose. The gunfight's not until the afternoon. We're safe until then."

They hurried away, several times glancing back at me.

Just then the sharp report of a gunshot slammed into the day, and just behind me, a window pane shattered. I ducked and looked around me, then at the broken glass.

What had just happened? Was I being fired upon?

"I might just kill you now." The words came from the roof of the building just across from me, and they snarled with contempt. "Ain't no sense in waiting for the afternoon."

"Are you serious?" My back had broken out in a sweat, and I yelled to the man, "You've got to be kidding. Was that a real bullet?"

"Jump lively." He laughed with a cackle, aimed his gun, and let off another shot that splintered the door I'd just exited.

It hit me in that moment. My clock. 18:74. That wasn't the time. It was the year. As the man fired off another shot, narrowly missing my feet, I threw myself back into the building and ran up the steps to my room. Once inside, I sat on the edge of the bed and picked up the clock. I turned a dial on the side and watched the numbers begin to change. I rotated it until it read the correct year, and I pulled the knob to set the alarm. I peeled off my old-fashioned clothing and climbed back into bed.

I covered my head with the blankets, and I tried not to shake with fear.

Please ring, alarm. This is life or death.

This was one time I didn't want to sleep in.

Accidental Hero

THE CAR SCREAMED to a halt.

It was an old-fashioned model, the sort with big metal bumpers. Four men wearing masks and carrying guns jumped out and ran into the nearest building. City Bank. I looked around as I slipped my skateboard into my backpack, certain alarms should be going off.

Or that law enforcement would come pouring around the corner to prevent a crime from being committed.

The street was deserted except for me. Through the narrow city vistas between the tall buildings, wispy clouds rolled past against a blue sky. An ordinary day.

Well, almost. The car was still running, with the two doors facing the building wide open. Like they intended to make a quick getaway. This was clearly a crime scene in the making, and it looked like it was up to me. I ran toward the car and was about to drop my backpack and grab the keys, when the jangling bells of the building's alarms broke the silence.

I jumped, startled. I didn't want to get shot!

As the doors to the building burst open to the accompaniment of gunfire, I ducked behind the rear bumper, working my way away from the open doors, and doing my best not to be seen.

I tensed my legs to run away, when I realized my backpack was tangled around the bumper. The car shifted as the men piled inside.

"No, no," I hissed and tried to release the catch on my pack. It was pulled tight by the tension, and it wouldn't give.

The car shifted into gear, and I knew my choices were limited. I whipped out my skateboard and leaped on, just as the car started to move.

It was a wild few moments, but I got the hang of keeping my balance, even though I was twisted sideways because of my backpack. Turning corners at the robbers' breakneck speed gave my heart a workout as sparks flew from the wheels of my skateboard.

The buildings in the city whizzed by with ferocious speed. I was glad there was no traffic on the road.

Finally, I calmed enough to remember my cell phone. I dialed 9-1-1.

"Emergency services. How may I help you?" The voice was calm and placating, as though speaking softly would solve any problem I might have.

"Help!" I yelled over the sound of my wheels whining at nearly sixty. The sun kept glinting on my phone's screen, blinding me. We hit a dip in the road, and I yelled, "Ouch!"

"Sir, no need to yell. Tell us your location."

"Everywhere! In the city somewhere."

"You must be more specific. What street signs are you near?"

Was she crazy? The signs were passing in a blur. I tried, though.

"Let me look. Third. Now we're passing Second. We're coming to—"

"Come, now, sir, you can't be at all three places."

"I'm at none of those places. I'm at Mockingbird and Broad. Scratch that, we just turned on Skelton Boulevard. Get the police here quick!"

"I'm sorry, sir. Where? You keep changing your location."

"I'm not doing it, lady. I'm just holding on for dear life."

That was about the truth of it, too. I looked around the side of the car to see that we were approaching the on-ramp to the freeway. My heart jumped into my throat, and I pictured eighty as the robbers raced for freedom.

My life was toast.

Then I heard sirens, but they didn't sound like they were coming this way. I spoke into the phone, yelling at the emergency operator.

"I think I hear police officers on the road."

"Nothing to do with you, sir. Let's see if we can pinpoint your location." She was so calm.

She had no idea how varied my location could be, and it was about to get much worse.

"It's everything to do with me! I'm with the robber's car. City Bank? I was there when it was robbed, and I'm tailing the car."

"Oh, my!" Her voice changed in tone, as if she was finally taking me seriously. "Don't lose them. I'll get the police on the line."

Lose them? I wished I could lose them. This was my life we were talking about.

About that time, the car sped up. I cringed. The on-ramp. Then the vehicle jumped, skipping over a curb on the opposite side, jerking me sideways. There was a screech of brakes—not ours!—and the car swerved back onto the feeder road. I nearly dropped my phone. Losing my skateboard would be worse, and I breathed a sigh of relief.

I yelled into the phone, "Anyone there?"

It seemed I must have gotten someone's attention, because a helicopter appeared overhead. A voice came over my phone telling me to not hang up, to keep the line open.

They explained before the ceremony when they awarded me the Citizen Service Medal that with my GPS signal, they apprehended the thieves with no problem. It was my bravery in holding onto that car that saved the bank nearly $20 million. They even called me a hero.

I didn't tell them the truth, that the strap of my backpack was stuck on the bumper. I didn't care about the Service Medal. The bank wanted to give me a big reward.

Heck, I'd let them believe the lie for that.

Plenty of Time

EVERYTHING STOPPED, frozen in time.

It was Saturday morning, and I was in the city for the day when bam, it happened. People were like statues all around me, families in cars, men on bicycles, babies in carriages. All lifeless. Not even their hair was blowing in the wind.

You've seen photographs that freeze action. People's hair is caught in the breeze fanning out from their heads. Flags still wave, even if they aren't really moving. Things like that.

This wasn't like that. The world hung limply around me, the tree branches in the park were stilled, and the water fountain on Fourth and Vine was glassy and smooth.

Not a puff of wind.

I don't guess hearts were beating inside all those people, although mine was pounding away. I was scared.

I guess some people would see this as an opportunity to explore. Go places you otherwise weren't allowed. After all, who would stop you? Even if they were conscious of you being there, they couldn't chase you. They couldn't even move.

After a couple of hours, the novelty began to wear off, and my fear subsided. I had sat in the park awhile, looking at the ducks standing on the shore, then I'd gotten curious and looked for the ones that usually swam in the lake. They'd drifted down by the floodgates where the overflow fed the stream down the hill. The water was still draining over the sluice, creating a current, so some things still moved.

I hoped no ducks had been feeding underwater when time froze for them. I didn't know if they could

drown, because they might not be breathing, but still. It was cringeworthy, even if they were just ducks. I looked but didn't see any. I also didn't see any fish, either floating or under the water. Or airplanes in the sky. What happened to them if they were flying? Did they drop to the ground? It was too much for me to figure out.

Finally hungry, and with the day warming up, I went inside a convenience store—Delray's Corner Market—and helped myself to a can of soda. Inside the cooler was still cold, and before I thought, I moved the can over the scanner, to no result. I pulled a card from my wallet and put it in the chip reader, wondering if this meant I didn't have to pay. Nothing. That told me something. The computer was frozen, too. I glanced back, thinking about getting out the soda. The light had come on in the cooler when I opened the door, so there was some electricity some-where, even if it was residual power in the lines.

A backup generator, perhaps? Or one of those wall-mounted powerpacks that store electricity to pre-vent power surges from damaging the machinery? It was a business, after all, with lots of machinery inside.

I tried the walk button on the corner, but the signs were dead. So, I walked anyway, getting cocky. I could do anything I wanted. Browse fancy shops, enter people's apartments, even borrow people's cars, if they'd start.

As I turned the corner was when I saw the girl.

Woman, I should say. Young, about my age, twenty-five or so. Not frozen, but window shopping, with her arm behind her neck, pulling her hair up before shaking her head and letting it fall. She had several paper bags with store logos on them over one arm, as though she'd been on a spending spree.

Except that you couldn't spend. I'd already seen that.

"Hey," I called, raising my arm and waving. It sounded loud in the stillness, like an intrusion into the silence. At first, she didn't respond, and I started to run her direction. "Hey, I'm glad I found you. I haven't seen anyone else alive all day."

She continued to browse, moving on into a shop, causing the door to ding, and letting it close behind her, like she hadn't heard me at all. I could see her inside, and I knocked on the glass. I tried the door, but it had one of those electric actuators on it, the self-closing kind, and it refused to budge.

I pressed my forehead to the glass and looked at my feet for a moment, then turned to the street. It was filled with people doing all sorts of things, though at the moment they were doing nothing. Maybe some of them were alive, too. I walked among them to see, waving my hand in front of their faces, all the while keeping my eyes on the store in case the woman came out again. Before long, I was darting one to another, faster and faster, wanting someone to blink.

I was across the street when the door dinged again. I looked at the shop to find the woman, and I could see the door swinging to. I didn't see her, though. Not then. I found her on Maple, still with her packages, frozen like the others.

That freaked my sense of self into another zone.

It's been six months, now. That's happened several times. I see people moving, but they don't see me. It's like we're on different planes of existence. Maybe when the world stopped, it left slices of time still in motion, and like the hands on a clock, they move around the world, animating people for a time then freezing them again.

I wonder if they know, if they can tell. If they can see me when they're frozen, like I see them when they're not.

There's one good thing in all this. Delray's still has power, and the cooler is always restocked. I get all the sodas I want, and I never have to pay.

Angel's Ghost

I HAD NEVER seen a ghost, not the real kind.

But like they say, there's a first time for every-thing.

My friend Angel and I were out—on Halloween, wouldn't you know—just riding around in my car, looking for some mischief. There wasn't much going on, since trick-or-treating is mostly banned. All the kids now go to those indoor things sponsored by civic groups or church organizations, leaving the streets clear for those of us who like to do the real pranks.

Tricks-not-treats, I like to say.

We had a trunk full of paint, and our

first trick was to burn old-man Johnson's car. It still wore a ghost from last Halloween, where our tags hadn't buffed out all the way. We gave it the Full Monty, the wheels, tires, and everything. Like a glowing Halloween pumpkin, we laughed, as we pulled away.

Angel wanted to go downtown, to do a gallery. I had a trunk full of paint, so I said sure. Maybe a heavens? Angel liked that. I had my climbing gear in the back floorboard, two sets like always, so we could be spur-of-the-moment if we wanted.

We'd need some fat caps, cause a heaven spot has to be painted big. I'd used up my last fat caps doing a fill on the Simmons Bridge. I had some at a stash spot I rent down on James, and I grabbed some extra rope while we were there. Angel pointed to where someone had toyed over one of my best tags, and I knew I'd have to come back and repair the damage. It was my pride at stake, and I couldn't let other artists see my work being disrespected by some newbie who didn't know better.

"Want to make a throw-up on the

way?" Angel grinned, shaking a can of paint just to tease me. He pointed to a building with patches where the owner had tried removing the unwanted graffiti.

"Leave it to you to bomb the whole neighborhood." I laughed, slamming the brakes and bringing the car to a stop. We looked around and saw so one, so we jumped out, and I opened the trunk. It was filled with new and partially used cans of spray paint, known as cannons.

Angel's a king in the world of graffiti artists. The best, able to burn anyone's style. He did an angel dress-up at Sixty-Sixth and Baker in tribute to his mentor when he was killed, and it's still there, it's so good. He carries a black book with all sorts of his latest ideas for burners and more complex pieces, especially for the galleries along the waterfront, where the paintings can stay up for months before they get massacred.

Me? I like to do hollows, especially over buildings with lots of glass. The "shells" or "outlines" let the people inside look out after I'm done, and sometimes my work doesn't get buffed so quickly.

I did the shells while Angel filled and added decorative detail. He snapped on a fat cap for the broad strokes, covering a wide swath with each motion of his arm. We took about ten minutes before we fell back in the car, laughing and tossing our cannons in the back, along with the various tips we'd used.

"What a burn," Angel chortled.

"Only because it's all been buffed." I slapped him on the chest with the back of my hand.

"Hope no *toys* ruin our work." A toy is when someone *tags over your stuff*. That's what once happened to a tag I'd done, an elaborate piece I'd spent nearly an hour on.

"They'll know better if I tag it." Angel jumped out of the car with a cannon in hand and scrawled his tag in a one-liner just at the edge of the piece so it didn't detract from the overall image.

"Let them bite that," he said, hard, as he fell back into the car. "Ain't nobody done a piece that good in a long time."

"They do, it's stealing, but they don't care about that. We'll have to keep a watch and cap the bite with a throw-up to remind them who's king." I was bobbing my head as I spoke, and I turned the key and revved the engine. I spun the wheels as we tore from the curb on the way deeper into downtown.

We drove around for a bit, finally deciding on the Walker Tower. About thirty stories, it had a setback at the twenty-eighth floor with a two-story glass front. It was clean and perfect for an end-to-end. The climbing gear, two backpacks filled with paint, and we'd be on our way. I parked in an alley so we wouldn't draw attention, and we started up the fire escape.

We began with a dress-up over the most accessible glass, filling in the space entirely. Whoever was inside wouldn't be able to see out, but at this height, our work might be left up for several weeks, perhaps even becoming a landmark. We could only hope. We had to don the climbing gear to get to the top half of the glass. We hadn't planned on one of my ropes getting tangled. We dropped over the side, and I made it just fine, but Angel was stuck at the top.

"Hey, Delco, I'm not moving. What's wrong with your gear?"

It was mostly dark, and I could see him, but not what had him stuck. I told him to climb back up. It was likely hung and needed to be unstuck.

He disappeared, and I began to paint. Again, I was putting up the shells, leaving Angel the fills. It was a good combination, each of us using the skills we were best at. About halfway through, I yelled up to him, "Angel, where are you, bro?"

"Can't . . . get . . . this rope . . . unstuck." He leaned over the top and waved. Then he called, "Got it!" and he came tumbling over the side.

That's when I saw him flying through the air. Yeah, Angel crashed into the glass, hitting his head at an odd angle, leaving blood streaming down the side of our half-finished piece. Before I could get to him, he was gone. I hauled him to the top, and before I carried him off the building, I completed our master-piece, domming his blood in with the paint.

It was a fitting tribute to a king who had become a master. Of course, several weeks later it was mas-sacred, buffed away by the city. I could always see it,

though, a ghost of Angel's last piece

reflecting in the glass when the sun caught it just right.

Angel's ghost. How appropriate was that?

Teddy Scare

MICKEY OPENED THE safe to find it empty.

Sweat ran in rivulets down his face, and his heart was a freight train in his neck. This was the last place the necklace could have been, and where he remembered putting it.

He fell heavily into a chair and stared at the black chasm in the wall. No one had the code, not even Sandra. Who could have opened it?

And emptied it? *Everything* was gone.

He stood, pushed the door to, and spun the lock. It was no good anyone finding out what he'd lost, and the anniversary party was tonight. Ten years. He wondered if he had time to get into the city and replace it.

He jumped at a knock on the door.

"A minute," he called, trying to control the rush of adrenalin surging though him. He wiped his face and adjusted his suit, glancing in the mirror to ensure his panic didn't show. Taking a deep breath, he pulled the door wide.

"Hi, Daddy." Chip, his two-year-old, wrapped his arm around Mickey's leg for a brief moment before running past him into the room. He carried his stuffed bedtime bear, the one with the zipper in the back for his pajamas, under one arm. He jumped on the office sofa and set the bear beside him, humming a childish tune that occasionally ended in a whispered number.

"Hey, Chip. Whatcha need?" Mickey walked to the window and looked outside before glancing at his watch. The sun was out, and the drive would take at least half an hour. He might be good on time, if he left right now.

"Teddy wants to play. Will you play with him?"

"I'm sorry, Chip. I don't have time.

Daddy has to run into the city." He smiled at the boy in apology and sat at his desk, pulling the drawers open for the tenth time, taking out his keys and just hoping he might see something he'd missed before.

"Why, Daddy?" Chip held up the bear to his father.

"Daddy's misplaced something for the party to-night, and Mommy will be really sad if Daddy doesn't get another one."

Mickey cringed. He shouldn't have said that. Chip was a memo machine. Everything he heard he repeated to anyone who would listen. As in, his mother.

"What did you lose, Daddy?" The boy clambered off the sofa and, dragging the bear behind him, walked to the desk. He put Teddy on top, adjusting his legs until he sat up, only leaning slightly to one side. "Can Teddy help you look?"

"Thanks, Teddy. Thanks, Chip." He patted the stuffed toy on the head, then tweaked his son's nose. "I don't think the little guy's gonna be able to help this time."

"Teddy always finds what I lose." Chip grasped the bear's leg and, with a change of focus, he ran from the room, his furry friend bobbing frantically at his side.

"There you are, hiding as always."

Mickey looked through the door to greet Sandra, in monstrous curlers, well on her way to preparing for the evening. Her collar touted a large, paper napkin, suggesting her makeup was in situ, or at least in the process.

"Not hiding. Just needing to run into the city for a bit." He smiled to ease the sting. She was always accusing him of running from his social responsibilities, and tonight had been his promise to prove her otherwise. No emergency office calls. No out-of-town trips. Nothing to make them late or otherwise interfere. The anniversary party came before everything else.

The necklace was the crux of all he'd planned, a gift she'd hinted at for the past six months.

"You can't, Mickey. Not today. You just can't." Her eyes narrowed, and her words took on a hurt tone.

"It's not work." He stood, palming his keys. He glanced at his watch. He could just make it, if he left now.

"No. It never is, is it?" She crossed her arms, all business now. "Just once, just this once, I thought you were putting me first. Besides, you need to pick up the babysitter this afternoon. It's Jasmine Ritter, Angeline's younger sister. Angeline has a date, and her sister doesn't drive."

"Right." He'd forgotten he was responsible for that, too. He squeezed the keys in his hand, working out the logistics in his head. If he picked up Jasmine on the way back from the city, if the traffic wasn't heavy . . . but he'd have to call the jeweler's from the car, although that was no problem.

Then Chip appeared as though by magic at Sandra's side, holding out Teddy toward Mickey.

"Can Teddy go? Teddy wants to help Daddy search."

"Search for what, Mickey?" Sandra's mouth was a tight line. "Just tell me that."

"Sorry, Sandra." Mickey laughed in what he hoped was a conciliatory manner, and he picked up Chip and kissed his wife on the cheek, as he stepped through the door. He called back, "It's nothing. The boy's right. Teddy and I have this handled. I'll have Jasmine here. Everything's fine."

It wasn't, though. Every second lost was, well, a second lost, and he couldn't afford to let this evening get away. In the kitchen, he set Chip on the counter and said, "Daddy's going out. What we said earlier is between Daddy, Chip, and Teddy. It's a surprise for Mommy, and she'll be sad if she finds out too soon."

"Okay, Daddy. Teddy wants to go with you."

"I don't think—"

"Pleease?" The small face twisted in dismay, then brightened when Mickey sighed and grabbed the bear.

"Sure, Son. I don't know what Teddy can do, but he can ride along."

"I want down, Daddy." Once on the floor, the boy ran off, happily reprising his song from earlier as he disappeared into the den.

It was only when Mickey was in the car with Teddy strapped in the passenger seat that Chip's song made sense to him. The boy had been on the sofa in his office when he'd put the necklace in the safe. Like he'd said, his son was a memo machine.

He could repeat anything, and Mickey liked to say the numbers aloud when he turned the lock.

He pulled the bear out of the seat belt and turned it over, unzipping the back. He laughed to see it stuffed with papers he recognized. He fished around to pull out a blue velveteen box with a jeweler's logo on top, the very one he'd been searching for. The boy had been singing the combination to his safe.

He slipped the box in his jacket pocket, leaned his head back, and closed his eyes, ecstatic with relief. He jumped when someone knocked on the glass.

He rolled down the window. "Yes, Sandra?"

"You're still going into the city after our discussion?" Her curlers were down, but the napkin still dressed her collar. She looked angry.

"Of course not. Teddy and I are headed to get Jasmine."

"Aren't you a bit early?" She fought a smile.

"It's our anniversary. It's never too early for the one I love."

"I love you, Mickey."

"I know." He smiled and rolled up the

window. Jasmine could sit in the back. For this trip, Teddy would be his honored guest for saving the day.

Changing Day

GREY AND OMINOUS, the castle stood on the hill.

Looking down across the small town, in the topmost window of the highest tower, stood a man. Except for the little flickering lights from across the valley, darkness ruled the night as far as he could see. Wind-driven snow littered the air, and winter would soon turn the landscape, creating an expanse of white roofs and smoking chimneys. Anonymity to the tenth degree. Everyone the same.

No difference between the masters and the servants, perfect weather for Changing Day.

Once a century, in the heaviest storm

of the season, when the bushes were mounded with snow, and the fireplaces were stoked and burning hot, the world turned topsy-turvy, upside down. Smiles turned into frowns, though for some, it was the other way around.

The Designer was the only one who didn't change on Changing Day. It was his duty to look down across the town and ensure that Changing Day came right on time, whether the residents of the town wanted it to or not.

***

"Andrew, come down for breakfast. You'll be late for school."

Andrew groaned, pulled his VR headset off, and yanked the earbuds from his ears. He'd been at the most exciting part of the scenario. All the vampires would turn into werewolves, and the werewolves into vampires.

"Andrew!"

"Okay, Mom. I'm coming."

He bounded down the stairs to find his breakfast on the table, steaming eggs and sausage, the sort with little mouse ears. He fell into his chair and reached for one.

"Did you wash your hands?" His mother leaned in from the laundry room. "Now, buddy."

"If you insist." He leaped up, turned on the water, and wet them down. They only left a small smudge when he dried them on the towel.

His game was all he could think of on the way to school. During math, he doodled what the werewolves would look like as vampires. In English, he drew the vampires with thick, bushy hair.

This game would be the best one anyone had ever played.

***

"John, is that design ready for post-production tweaks?"

John groaned and pulled his VR headset off. He looked at his boss with irritation and barked, "It would be if you didn't interrupt every five minutes. I've got the boy designing what he thinks the Changing Day will do to the vampires and the werewolves. This takes time, you know. If it looks like familiar images people have seen before, they won't pay for the game."

"No Lon Chaney, then." His boss snickered. "Thank God for that."

"Thank me for that." The moment was spoiled, though. John's concentration was broken, and it would take some time for him to get his head around how the boy felt and what the boy's designs would look like. And it had to be realistic and lifelike in the simulation. He slipped on the headset and skipped back to an earlier scene.

***

Inside the castle, darkness had started to descend. Oil-soaked torches lined the hallways, and servants tittered with anticipation. Changing Day was a story out of legend, a tale a hundred years old, one that had become a bedtime ritual, but that no one alive had experienced.

Each servant hoped it was true.

Of course, the Lords and Ladies had a different take on the matter. They frowned and muttered each time a servant seemed uppity. They had lived a life of luxury and prestige. They didn't want to give up that.

The Lords bared their fangs each time one of their bushy-haired servants drew near.

***

"What's that, Andrew?"

It was the last period of the day. Science. They were in the lab, and his teacher tapped his drawing paper with her fingertips.

"Nothing, Miss Lindenmeier." He tried to slip it into his satchel.

"It looks like something to me." She turned it to reveal bloody fangs on a furry werewolf face, and she shivered as she folded it in half and tucked it in her pocket. "Don't let me see it again."

Andrew was compelled, however. Something about creating the perfect creatures for his video game had given him a sense of urgency he'd never known before. He couldn't wait for the school day to end.

When the teacher moved on, he slipped out another page and started a new design.

This one would be scarier than the

last.

***

"John?"

John tossed his VR headset aside and barked, "What now?"

"Are you playing the part of the scenario designer again with the gaming system?"

"Sheesh," John muttered. "You take all the fun out of my job." He slipped the headset back on and picked up the controls.

***

Inside Gaming Systems, INC's massive mainframe computer, the Artificial Personality Generator had created a faulty Virtual Reality loop, cycling from werewolves and vampires to a schoolboy, to a very lifelike and frustrated scenario designer. It seemed there was no way out that resolved the faulty loop with any sort of reasonableness. Systems were running at full speed, and one processor had already approached critical temperatures.

As a last-ditch effort to salvage the game, the APG reset the John parameter, had him whip his headset off and push his chair back, and say, "I'll make some changes in the set-up and start again tomorrow."

As he stepped away from his desk, the APG in the mainframe accessed a sister system running a similar but not identical scenario, and its cooling fans began to spin faster and faster.

***

Grey and ominous, a prison stood on the hill.

Looking down across the chain link covered prison yard, in the topmost window of the highest tower, stood a man. Except for the glowing lights from security monitors, darkness ruled the night. Wind-driven snow littered the air, and winter would soon turn the landscape, creating an expanse of white as far as the eye could see.

No difference between the guards and the prisoners, perfect weather for Changing Day. The Warden's duty was to ensure Changing Day came right on time, whether the men and women within its walls wanted it to or not.

The Straggler

"AM I IN HEAVEN? What's happened to me?"

I asked the question aloud, but there was no answer. That made sense, as there was no one around that I could see. Only tons of fluffy clouds.

Oh, and I had wings. That was my best clue. Where else did one receive wings, if not in heaven?

I looked over the edge of my cloud, getting a bit ill to my stomach. I've never had a constitution for heights. Even walking up the stairs gives me the jeebies, unless the railing's solid.

My head spun, and I pulled away, collapsing into my cloud like it was a giant, white beanbag, only softer. It was the earth down there, about a million miles away. All green, and divided neat-like into farming squares of different colors.

I thought of my family, Mom, Dad, and Gramps. Did they know where I was? I doubted it. I began to wonder how I got here, and whether they were likely to be here with me. You know, like in a car wreck where everyone is killed.

It might have happened.

I didn't remember us going out together, but we might have. Possibly, although we usually didn't.

A house explosion? Like with natural gas? It was conceivable, but I remembered that we were all electric.

Maybe Gramps went postal, and he shot all of us. That made me laugh. I couldn't imagine Gramps postal. Anyway, I had full health insurance, so I'd be in the hospital now, even if he did. Gramps is a really lousy shot with a rifle.

"Hey, anyone!" I yelled the words, hoping to get a response. I peered at the different clouds, just then noticing that they were moving around like real clouds. I looked around me, wondering what would happen if my cloud disappeared. Sometimes they did that. Would I fall to the ground? Oh, right, I had wings . . . *that I'd never used.*

My cloud began to vibrate, and I noticed a rumbling sound growing quickly louder.

"Hey, is someone paying attention to this?" I stood and yelled it out. Someone had to be somewhere. Didn't they?

Just then, right under my feet, a 747 tore by at a phenomenal speed, ripping the cloud right from under me.

"Yikes," I yelped, as the air cleared around me. By then, the airliner had disappeared into the distance, leaving no more than a thin contrail to show where it had been.

I began to tumble, and before I knew it, I was flapping my wings, as though I'd been doing it all my life.

Rather, all my death.

After an hour or so, with no place to land, I began to tire. By then, the sun had slipped to the far side of the globe, and it had started to get dark.

Seeing the terminator line sweep across the planet, turning day into night, was impressive. Lights flickered on, more and more, the darker it got. It seemed strangely cheerful, like watching the Northern Lights in Alaska, except I was way up in the stratosphere. I was surprised to see how bright it was, especially along the coastlines.

I thought of my gramps' beach house. It would be dark this time of the year. That made me sad. I wanted it to be included in the happy lights. I searched just outside Vancouver, wondering if I could fly that far before I gave up, but it wasn't completely dark there. Anyway, thin clouds had started to put some drag into my flight. I hoped they thickened enough I could stop and rest for a time.

I was distracted by a bright light moving through the sky really fast. It zigzagged around a few times, as if searching. I decided that it was too bad I was dead. I could definitively prove that UFOs were real, because by the flight pattern, this was clearly one. If I had my cell phone and could take a picture, I could sell it to the National Enquirer and make a fortune.

Then, if I had my cell phone, I wouldn't have to yell into the clouds to see if anyone was nearby. I could call 9-1-1 and let them know I was here and needed a rescue.

Angel wings and all. Wouldn't that go down well?

I guess I must have fallen into the UFO's search pattern, because after about ten minutes, it zipped my direction, coming really fast. The clouds had thickened up by then, and I was resting my wings, with my feet on a not-very-solid cloud. When I shifted position too fast, my feet tended to slip, so I was holding really still.

When it got close, I saw it wasn't a UFO at all. It was a glowing chariot with a white-bearded, robed man holding the reins.

"Jesus?" I called out, as I waved my hand.

"Hardly," he laughed. "Yeshua is at a camp meeting in Australia. He's hoping to be back before dark, though they tend to go to all hours there."

"Sorry, God," I apologized.

"No, no!" He really laughed at that, holding his belly. "Yahweh is at orientation. I'm here for stragglers."

"Oh?" I was pleased to hear that. "You must be St. Peter."

"I wish." He held out a hand. "Moshe, of Exodus fame. You know me as Moses. Come aboard. It seems you got left behind."

"Left behind?' Did that mean I didn't get to go to heaven?

"Shush." Moses held a finger to his lips. "I won't tell if you don't. You slipped off the back of Elijah's chariot, and no one noticed. I hope to get you back before Yahweh discovers you're gone. It doesn't look good when we leave someone behind, even accidentally."

"Before we go, I have to ask an important question. How did I die?" If anyone would know that, Moses would. I shook with anticipation.

"Your health insurance was cancelled, just before you got stung by a wasp, and you were out of Epi-Pens."

"My health insurance was cancelled?" I was incredulous.

"Sorry, but when it's your time to go, it's your time to go." Moses shrugged.

I was disappointed. My death should have been more exciting. My chariot ride to heaven made up for it, though. If anything, Moses drove at a spine-snapping million miles an hour.

I whooped with excitement all the way.

Cruising for a Bruising

CLOSER AND CLOSER it came.

It was getting bigger and bigger, and soon it filled the sky. When it blocked the sun was like the last time I saw the total eclipse. The wind cooled, the birds went silent, and all the street lights came on.

My heart pounded as I asked the question leaping out in my mind: Was the moon falling?

It was possible, but not probable. I searched for Mares Nubium, Fecunditatis, or Tranquilitatis, all to no avail. Nada. There was nothing there that looked the least familiar, even though I hadn't studied the moon since my university days, so I could be missing something. The surface wasn't smooth, like a baby's behind, whatever it was. It just wasn't the moon, I was pretty certain. An alien ship? Like in *Independence Day*? Or maybe in the second movie, because that ship was even bigger, covering a quarter of the planet.

I pulled my jacket collar tighter and stepped inside my office. If the aliens were attacking, there was no use in me getting a cold in the process. If there were negotiations to be performed, at least a couple of us humans had to be in prime condition. To be on the safe side, I peeled off my jacket and draped it on a chair, before dropping to the floor to do a dozen pushups. As I lifted my body on number twelve, I was getting energized, and I decided a dozen one-handers would be good. A dozen on each side.

I'm a bit of a fitness nut, you see. Pushups. Knee bends. Run a mile . . . or two. When the weather permits . . . or if it doesn't, I find a way.

I even did boxing for a spell, until I had to have my nose fixed. That kept me from doing my pushups for a week, because it tried to bleed when I was on my face for too long, and I wasn't going there. Missing my pushups was no good, in my book.

I was just brushing my hands on my pants—having finished all thirty-six pushups and a dozen sit-ups—when I noticed a commotion outside the door. I looked to see people running down the sidewalks and even spilling over into much of the street. One woman carried a Macy's bag, and when she collided with another pedestrian and the bag tore, she didn't even stop to retrieve her fallen merchandise.

That's when I knew this was serious.

The trees in the median were whipping by that time. The day had been warm, and the sudden cooling had set up a temperature differential. Air was moving from the high-pressure area underneath the thing to warmer, low-pressure areas somewhere that the sun still shone.

If the whole earth hadn't been covered by the obnoxious thing in the sky.

I put my jacket back on, and just to be sure—since I remembered how cold it had grown—I pulled my overcoat on over that. Flipping the collar up, I gripped the doorknob, and holding tight (because of the wind), I thrust the door open. Closing it firmly, I stepped outside. I faced the direction the people were running *from,* and I understood.

Independence Day, here we come.

The thing overhead—a real, alien ship, I could now see—hovered just over the tops of the buildings. And get this, a hole had opened in the ship, from which they'd extended a giant stairway from the bottom, and this bug-like creature was sauntering down it casually as you please.

It was nearly at street level, and it was clicking these giant claws in what could only be described as a jazz rhythm.

Like, cool, man.

Only it wasn't cool, because all these guns dropped out of these turrets about that time, swiveling around and startling me, and I dropped into a half-crouch, ready to dart back into my office at the least provocation.

I didn't want to die, after all, even if this was the best watercooler story I'd ever experienced in my entire life.

Then the creature pointed at me, and with a buggy, raspy voice, said, "You. I require your assistance. You must negotiate for your world's continued existence."

It was a distinctly male voice.

I looked around to make sure he was talking to me, and as by that time, everyone else had disappeared, I accepted that he was.

"Okay," I called back.

"Come closer, puny human." He motioned with one of his claws, the other still clicking a smooth jazz tune.

Puny human. That insult got under my skin, I'll tell you that. I did move closer. It was all those guns. What choice did I have? When I got face to face with him, I was surprised to see that he was about my size. He'd looked so much bigger from fifty feet over my head.

"I will take your planet for my own," the bug said, still clicking those claws, like this was a scene in a musical, "unless you prove to me that you can stop me."

Arrogant so-and-so, I thought. I didn't

see how we could stop him, with that giant ship bristling with guns, and I shrugged.

"It's as I thought," he said, to a jazz accompaniment, and I'm certain he laughed. He sneered, "You humans are wimps through and through."

I grew hot. The first insult was out of line, but this was too much; and I remembered from the movie how the pilot punched one of the aliens in the nose. I balled up my fist and let him have it. He squeaked, turned, and ran up the ramp as fast as he could.

We never saw that ship again, and I want to warn all the aliens out there. Come to our world and make fun of us, and you're cruising for a bruising.

Do it a second time, and that's exactly what you're going to get.

Garden Gnomes

CHAD WANDERED through the house.

He was seeking any form of distraction to avoid the inevitable doom, and he'd refused to look out the windows, so far. The weather had changed that morning, and with the rain pelting the glass, a sense of foreboding had overcome him.

Why did it feel like he was nearing the gallows?

The phone rang, and he picked it up.

"Chad Fellowes. How may I help you?"

"Randolph, from across the street. Have you been watching the gnomes in your yard?" He sort of giggled, like it was a big deal.

"Yeah, Randolph. I know about the gnomes. What are they doing now?" Chad walked to the front window, dreading what he'd find. The gnomes always came out when the rain started, and they always left a royal mess to clean up.

Chad took hold of the fabric, preparing to pull the curtains open. It was easy to say they always came out and left everyone's yard a mess, but that wasn't true for all the yards in Topeka. Mostly they were in his yard, because, when they first appeared, he'd been the first one to call the exterminator, and that had gotten on the gnomes' nerves.

Now they hung around in his yard just to torment him.

Chad pleaded nightly for it not to rain. Sunshine was the gift from the Almighty that said he was loved and appreciated. A bright, hot day was the only kind that mattered to Chad, anymore.

He pulled the curtain back and at first didn't see anything. Then he noticed the tree at the corner of the drive. He cursed, a small sound under his breath, but it was there, nonetheless. His rosebud tree.

The little buggers had uprooted his beautiful rosebud, turned it upside down, and buried the branches with all the flowers, leaving the roots extending into the air.

There was no way the tree would live like that, although, with the gnomes, they were magical with the garden. If it could be grown, they could grow it. Take Mrs. Higginbotham's petunias. Last fall, they'd moved them all into her gutters, and they were still blooming profusely, a whole winter on. It seemed to Chad that a winter in the gutters, even for cold-loving flowers like petunias, would kill any plant.

Nope, those gnomes knew exactly what they were doing.

He couldn't figure out the point in planting the rosebud upside down. Then he noticed the shrubs outside the window were done the same way. That was enough! He ran into the front yard, sticking to the sidewalk, because the gnomes had been known to remove all the dirt under the grass, leaving a void that would swallow a man whole.

He came to a stop at his mailbox. All that was left was the pole, covered with concrete, of course, where it had been turned upside down. Drat! Something else to move, otherwise, the mailman wouldn't be able to deliver his mail.

"Chad, you got it under control?"

He turned to see Randolph on his porch with a hand raised to wave.

"Yeah, Randolph. I might leave it this way for a time. Trendsetter. That's me." Chad laughed, but he didn't feel it. Instead, it was a gut-wrenching sensation that made him want to dig the little suckers out of the ground and throttle every single one. He tried to wriggle the mailbox, but the thing was solid in the dirt like stone.

It started to rain harder, and Chad gave up and headed inside. He watched for the gnomes. They were quick and hard to spot. Once, he'd set up a motion-activated camera on a rainy night, recording at least three. One had an orange cap, one green, and the last one, blue. Today, he hadn't noticed any flashes of color before racing to the door, and he dismissed it from his mind. The weather station on the television had predicted sunshine for the morning, and that meant Chad could get out and undo some of the damage. It took a lot of work just to maintain the status quo, but it was better than letting the gnomes take over.

That night, Chad was awakened repeatedly by the little guys' activities. They were banging away something fierce. Chad's bed shook a time or two, and once, he almost got up to lean out the window to yell at them to STOP WHAT THEY WERE DOING. He didn't, though. It would irritate them, and the next rainstorm, they would be more industrious than ever.

The next morning, when Chad stood from bed, he felt dizzy, like he had been on a merry-go-round, sort of lightheaded. The light from around the blinds was odd and colorful. He didn't go to the windows, though. He didn't want to know what the gnomes had been up to during the night. If all his bushes and his redbud tree had been upside down yesterday, think what they could have gotten up to overnight. It had rained the entire time.

It was stepping out the door to head to work that made Chad realize he wasn't in Kansas, anymore. It was barely light, and the sky was overcast; but the clouds were a neon green, and he could see his mailbox just fine. It was right-side up, and his redbud was blooming profusely—from the branches. Even his shrubs were turned the correct direction.

What was odder was Randolph's house. All he could see was the foundation—from the underside! Plumbing pipes stuck into the air, dripping water that flowed into the sky. Randolph's trees? Just the roots were showing. Glancing down the street, all the other houses were the same. He turned back to his house to see it normal and serene.

Except for the sky now turning cotton-candy pink . . . and the three gnomes that climbed out of his redbud tree.

"What have you done?" Chad yelled in a very undiplomatic voice.

The orange one said, "We've invited you . . ."

The green one continued, ". . . to our side . . ."

And the blue one finished, ". . . of the world."

Then there was a neon green flash of lightning, and purple rain fell from the sky. The gnomes cheered and scattered down the street.

Chad fled for his house.

Now? Chad rarely gets to enjoy the sunshine. The garden gnomes love the rain, and wouldn't you know it? On the gnomes' side of the world, it rains almost every day.

Dinner Date

FELICITY'S SURPRISE TURNED to dismay.

Peeking through the window, she saw a giant birthday cake coming up the sidewalk, followed by a baby dinosaur and a unicorn.

"Mike," she called, dropping the blinds and turning back into the room.

"Yes, Sweetie?" He stepped in from the bathroom, adjusting his tie. They were headed on a dinner date to Delmonico's, the finest dining establishment in the Oklahoma Panhandle. He had on his new boots, with the ostrich uppers, and a braided leather belt. His beard was freshly trimmed, and he boasted a smile.

"Should there be a dinosaur in our yard?" Felicity hadn't dressed yet, but her makeup was done, and she was in her best slip. Her freshly pressed outfit was hanging on the back of the door, with her black pumps just at the side. She sported irritation at the corners of her eyes.

"A dinosaur? Come, now, Felice." Mike turned back to the bathroom and lifted a comb to run it though his hair. He'd touched up his temples, and his hair wasn't laying just right. "Dress, Dear, if you want to be on time."

Their reservation was at five, and you did have to have a reservation at Delmonico's. Otherwise, you were turned away.

"But what about the unicorn?"

"There's one of those, too?" A chuckle accompanied Mike's question. "What are we in, a fairy tale, now? Chop, chop, Sweetheart."

"And if there's a birthday cake coming up the sidewalk, what would you say to that?" She lifted her dress from its velveteen-encrusted hanger and turned it wrong side out. She lifted it over her head and let it slide down her arms until it covered most of her, neck to knees. "Zip me, if you will."

"Certainly." He set the comb on the counter and turned, expertly grasping the small, metal protuberance with a practiced hand and doing her up.

"About the birthday cake," she reminded him.

"I'd eat it right up and think I'd had a special treat." He smiled and tweaked her nose with the tips of two fingers.

"You are a horror. I think you're about to have that special treat." She hoped they could get the car out. If the dinosaur decided to encamp in their drive, it would be difficult to make it move. She slipped on her shoes and headed out the door. It looked like it would be one of those nights.

***

They made it to Delmonico's in time, barely.

The dinosaur hadn't been in the drive. Heaven knew, it could have been on the roof, by then. It was the unicorn in the way. The cake had parked itself half on and half off the grass, and the glittering animal was licking icing from one side.

Felicity suggested backing into it and nudging it out of the way, but Mike would have none of it. It was a *unicorn,* wasn't it? The first seen in the Panhandle, although they were as common as blackberries in the East. They were forced to wait until it licked one side of the cake clean and moved on. It had icing on its horn that sparkled in the afternoon light.

Their real time-cruncher came on 287 into Guymon. A flock of pterodactyls descended on the highway. Mike mused that there had been an abundance of Easter bunnies out last time he was in Guymon, and he supposed the dacs, as they'd become known, had uncovered a warren of underground burrows. "Clear the little demons out, I should say. They eat the native grass to the roots, and the whole place goes to rot and ruin."

The dacs scattered when a troll came wandering by. Trolls fed on anything they could catch and break, the reason Mike and Felicity's car had an armored cage. Trolls would eat people, too, given the chance.

There'd been a rise of troll sightings

down in the Grasslands, but they mostly stayed in Texas.

At least they were moving again, giving them just enough time to make it to the restaurant. The specialty of the evening was pureed Dodo soup and sautéed pygmy mammoth, a real treat, even for the most discerning diners. Their waiter fluttered around, delivering each course with charming aplomb, his multicolored diaphanous wings stirring up just enough of a breeze to counter the thick, Oklahoma heat.

"We've had a fine evening, haven't we, Felice?" Mike kissed his wife on the cheek as they exited the door.

"I'm stuffed, although I shouldn't complain. No one forced me to order an extra serving of firebird fillets." She patted her stomach and let out a small belch. They had been served on a bed of rice and greens, and she hadn't been able to resist. Mike had declined, as habaneros were hot enough, in his opinion. Who needed to up the ante with firebird flesh? It was truly hot as fire.

They'd both laughed at that.

On the way home, they were forced to detour through Hardesty, because a three-headed dragon was terrorizing a truck stop in Hooker. Mike wanted to drive up and see, as it was a first for Oklahoma, but Felicity was tired, and besides, the firebird had her stomach a bit bloated. She really needed to get home.

All in all, it turned out to be a good evening. They even took in a special view of the northern lights flickering across the Oklahoma sky, although they saw them most nights these days. To end things perfectly, the unicorn had finished off most of the cake, allowing them to pull directly into their garage.

It was Mike and Felicity's best dinner date of the summer.

The Belly of the Beast

BANG! BOOM! CRASH!

What was the professor doing in his lab? I tumbled down the stairs, nearly tripping on the third step where the metal edging was worn, and I tore down the corridor toward the belly of the beast.

Heh, heh, that's a joke of mine . . . *belly of the beast*. Most people don't find it funny, but as the university had retained me to aid the professor in *dinosaur research*, well, *belly of the beast* . . . still funny, at least to me. If we do crack this DNA thing, a lot of people might wind up in the *belly of the beast*.

I see you're not laughing, so I guess

you're not into macabre humor. You know, *The Cask of Amontillado*, and other Poe fiction like that. Running down that corridor, you might think I was hoping for a real, living dinosaur in the professor's lab, what with my "belly of the beast" joke, but no, I've seen all those dinosaur movies, and they peg one thing perfectly: Dinosaurs eat people. Quickly, slowly, in small bites, or all in one gulp. No one's telling those beasts to "slow down and enjoy your dinner. You don't want indigestion, do you?" If they did, they might become the after-dinner mint, er, make that *after-dinner meat*.

Anyway, I reached the door to the professor's lab—which was open by the way—and I leaned in. I couldn't see anyone at first, but I heard hard breathing, so I knew someone was inside.

"Professor, you in here?" I didn't go in, not because I didn't have permission, but because I'd heard the bang, the boom, and the crash that had followed. And I knew the professor. His motto was "give it a try and see what happens." What happens hasn't always been pretty, and at times, barely survivable. I didn't want barely survivable. I wanted tomorrow and the next day and the day after that.

"Up here," his frightened voice whispered.

"Why are you whispering?" I whispered back.

"So she doesn't get me." The professor replied. "Keep your voice down and bring me the stepladder."

She? I looked up to find the professor on the top of a supply cabinet. His face was blackened and his hair sticking up on end, which explained the bang. The boom and crash? I was sure we'd get to those later. I did notice a long, red slash that started on his neck and blazed up one side of his face.

"Okay, professor. Sure. You do know the stepladder is in the storage closet, and that's on *the other side of the lab*." I hissed my final words intently. I wanted him to know that me getting the stepladder was a really bad idea if he was afraid of something getting him and it was still in the room.

Maybe not so bad for him, but likely really bad for me. When the professor's around, things can go sideways without much warning.

"And you're young enough to be my grandson. Help your old grandpop out, won't you, sonny?"

That's the other side of the professor, the reason I continue to work with him, even though he often risks my life and limb. He can crack a smart comeback with aplomb, and it gets to me every time.

"Yeah, why not? I don't need my extra leg. What would I do with it, run a marathon? Keep an eye out, professor. I'm going in."

"No thanks, I'll keep my eyes in my head, the better to see the boogie man with. You run on three, and I'll let you know if she's coming after you."

I'm supposed to feel better hearing that? From the *dinosaur creator*? I didn't want to know more, whether he'd turned a freshly minted dinosaur loose, because I might not enter the lab at all.

As I dashed through the open space, I did notice deep marks in the floor *the size of my arm.* Golly, I thought. Professor, what have you been working on? It was the scrambling noises behind the storage cabinets that really got my feet to moving. I pictured a velociraptor, maybe a pterodactyl, or even a baby T-rex. They all have claws, don't they? Or at least teeth. Maybe teeth could do that type of damage . . . who knows?

Then it hit me, I'm in the belly of the beast. I'm the one who knows. Of course they have teeth that could do that type of damage.

I did manage the stepladder. It got stuck halfway open as I pulled it from the storage closet. I heard something screech, and a glass specimen jar across the room shattered on the floor as I tried to close the ladder, and I thought, heck, not doing that, and I held the ladder in one hand and started to run the professor's direction with the legs of the ladder bumping along after me.

"Hurry," the professor yelled, apparently no longer caring if he was overheard or not. "She's coming back. I'm too young to die!"

So am I, I thought, but I didn't say it. I was too busy running for my life . . . with a stopover at the professor's hiding place atop the supply cabinet . . . with a stepladder I might have already broken as I pulled it from the supply closet.

The professor slid down that ladder like a fireman coming down a firehouse pole. The screeching was louder, and the storage cabinets on the far side of the room had started to shake. Something—whatever the professor had created—was about to come through, over or under, and it seemed she—if the professor was correct—wanted us.

We fell through the door just as we heard one of the supply cabinets tumble face down onto the floor, scattering the contents across the room, and creating a raucous explosion of noise. The shrieking of the creature in attack mode and coming our way only made the pandemonium worse.

I held the door shut while the professor inserted his ID card and the door locked and sealed the creature in. I tried to ignore the banging on the door as I slumped and pushed my hair back from my face. I gave him a hard look and let my frustration and fear burst from me.

"What creature did you bring to life in there?"

"Creature? That's not the half of it. It's my ex-wife. I forgot to mail the alimony check."

I stared at him a moment, thinking, what the hey? Then, after a moment, we both started laughing at how scared we'd been.

We'd have to let her out eventually, but for a time, we decided to let the old dinosaur have a good go at the door. The building's cafeteria was one floor up, and I'd missed lunch for this. Today, the professor could pay.

Merlin

I WOKE UP with a start.

Something was in my room. I couldn't see it, but it was definitely there. I could *feel* it, under my skin and in my thoughts. I pulled the covers to my chin, shaking in fear.

The wardrobe doors opened, and a green mist came pouring out.

"Yikes," I chirped, in a squeaky voice, before I remembered that I was hiding under my comforter.

"Yikes is right," a voice rumbled, as a hand grabbed my ankle and pulled me into the mist, through my wardrobe door, and into the greatest summer vacation adventure of my life.

Now, I know what you're thinking. It didn't have to be much of an adventure to be the greatest one of my life. I was only thirteen, and I'd never done much, except fall off the diving board at the county pool one July, bang my head, and get resuscitated by Stephanie, the lifeguard. That was a pretty big deal, at least in my world.

The mist in the wardrobe was better.

Think of Alice in Wonderland. When she falls through the rabbit hole, all sorts of strange things begin happening to her. She shrinks and she grows, she cries a sea of tears, and she meets a grinning cat.

My adventure was weirder than that.

You see, when I was pulled through my wardrobe, I didn't go anywhere, or so I thought at first. I woke up back in my own bed.

Yes, with the comforter tucked under my neck and sleep boogers in the corners of my eyes.

I yawned and stretched and threw back the covers. It was when I stepped out of bed that I knew something was different.

I didn't have a floor.

Rather, I had one, it just wasn't there. I looked down to find clouds under my feet.

Now, I hadn't become an angel, because I didn't have wings, and I really needed to use the bathroom, something I don't think angels worry too much about. There was a floor, I suppose, I just couldn't touch it, even though I didn't fall through when I stood up.

Sort of like an air floor. You know, when air pushes on you, and it moves you around. Except this air wasn't moving, more like just holding me in place.

Then I saw another bedroom floating by underneath me. The boy was wearing his pajamas, and he waved at me. I waved back. Weird. He was standing on an invisible floor, too, with a video remote in his hand.

He had a Virtual Reality helmet on, and I wondered how he could see me.

"Because you're in my screen, doofus."

The voice reverberated in my ears, and something punched me on the shoulder. I looked down, and the

kid was punching the air about shoulder

height. Then he aimed his remote my direction, and a green light shot my way, forming a circle on the air that made up my floor. The circle blinked, and he was there, standing beside me. I looked into his room, and sure enough, he wasn't there.

"How'd you do that?" I stepped back. This was my room, and strangers shouldn't be able to just teleport themselves inside.

"You can do it, too." He grinned. I couldn't see his eyes, but the rest of his face was clearly visible. He reached a hand toward something, although there wasn't anything there. Then, there was, and he was holding a second VR helmet that had appeared out of nowhere. He held it out to me. "Here, put this on."

I did, and bam, everything changed. We were still in my room, with the clear floor, but the boy had a face, now. He reached out a hand to shake.

"I'm Arthur. Glad to meet you. This must be your first time."

"First time?" I shook his hand, but I didn't understand his question. First time for what?

"Virtual reality. With the helmet." He

reached a fist to my face and tapped. He didn't touch me, as his knuckles never got closer than about four inches away, but I heard a distinct thunk, thunk, thunk sound. It was the helmet, and he was tapping on it. I figured out that right away.

"How do I control it?"

"Ha, ha! I forgot." He reached into nothing again, and he pulled out a controller. He pressed it into my hand. "It's on. Just squeeze it."

I did, and things began to happen. A green box appeared around my room, then disappeared when I released my grip. I aimed it, like Arthur had done, to see a light shoot out. A circle appeared in the distance. With a touch, I teleported there. A circle appeared beside me, and then Arthur was there.

"Cool," I said. "Where can we go?"

"Anywhere," he replied with a grin. "By the way, I'm Arthur. Arthur Pendragon." He held out his hand again.

"Merlin," I said. "Merlin Ambrosius. Where to, next?"

"I know where they have this cool

round table where all these knights get together. I think we'll have lots of fun . . ."

We didn't come home for a hundred years. We got to do magic stuff, kill dragons, and save a beautiful lady.

When I went back to school the next fall, we studied the story of King Arthur. It's funny the magician's name is the same as mine. Here's the best part. I got a really good grade, and that's the hardest class in eighth grade. Like I told the teacher, I didn't have to study a bit.

I'd already lived it all.

Before you close the book . . .

Did you like these stories?
Do you want to read more?
Look for **Volume 2** of

The Electric Minute

Coming Out Spring/Summer 2018

You can also find more books by Farley Dunn at:

 THREE SKILLET
www.ThreeSkilletPublishing.com